Leather Heights, Toronto, Canada

Kinky Tales from Hogtown

Leather Heights, Toronto, Canada

Kinky Tales from Hogtown

Edited by Youkali Youkali

Cuir & Queer
Toronto, 2013

The image on the cover is a combination of two pictures. The background picture *Toronto Night Skyline from Center Island Ferry* is by Marcus Obal and is licensed under Creative Commons. The foreground picture is by Eye of the Storm and is used with permission.

ISBN 978-0-9919257-0-4

CONTENT

ACKNOWLEDGEMENTS

This anthology was created as a fundraising activity by Youkali Youkali, Ms. Leather Toronto 2013. Every year, members of the Heart of the Flag Federation[1] (producers of Toronto Bound and the Toronto Leather Pride Title Competitions) raise funds to support charities within the sexual minorities' communities they serve and represent. In 2013, the beneficiary is the Canadian Lesbian and Gay Archives (CLGA). Founded in 1973, the CLGA has grown to become the second-largest LGBT archives in the world[2]. All proceeds from sales of this book during Youkali's title year will directly go to the CLGA, and thereafter to HOTF's charity of choice.

I would like to thank all the contributors to this anthology, who put their time and energy into making it a success: all the writers and visual artists, both professional and amateur, who submitted their work; Sarah Pie, who helped me throughout the process; and especially Andrea Zanin, who edited the whole book. I would also like to extend my gratitude to the

HOTF's Board of Governors for backing me throughout this project, and to my fellow titleholders Robert Miller, Mr. Leatherman Toronto 2013; Peter Rex, Mr. Rubber Toronto 2013; and Pup Ego, Toronto Puppy 2013. Their support makes all the difference.

Youkali Youkali
Ms. Leather Toronto 2013

---

1. I couldn't resist putting in a footnote or two for those that fetishize the scholarly style. HOTF's website is: http://hotfftoronto.com/
2. Learn more about the CLGA at: http://www.clga.ca/.

INTRODUCTION
A Baroque Castle
and a Phallic Monument

Youkali Youkali

In *The Pornographic Imagination*, Susan Sontag — who was trying to study porn and erotica with a critical approach but was obviously partial to the latter and had reservations about the former — said the action of porn is set in an "ahistorical dreamlike landscape," that is, space is of little importance in porn. This leaves one wondering what kind of porn (and erotica) she had read exactly — for isn't it the opposite? Doesn't space make the story? I don't know about your experience of this, but for me, the place where a hot scene occurs in fiction is essential to my understanding of the whole set-up; it helps set the table, and it plays an important part in how the scene develops and whether it does the trick for me.

When it comes to kinky porn, space seems even more important. I remember reading the Marquis de Sade and drawing little stick people in order to picture how the characters were located in space. And also, while writing about a kinky scene, using ragdolls to make sure whether a body or bondage position were realistic (my personal kinky history started with Barbies, but that's another story).

Space is closely related to potential fantasies, and specific places are linked to specific scenes: an airport hall, where the two strangers can go have sex in the accessible washroom stall; an empty parking lot, where the consenting subject can be abducted by partners in crime and moved to another location for further use; a natural setting, where it's time to get down and dirty. Some places are inseparable from their authors and books. It is hard to think of the Marquis de Sade's stories (him again!) without picturing castles where poor innocent virgins are held captive. Lady Chatterley's lover would not behave the same way (and nor would the lady) if the story were set, let's say, in the Far West instead of the English countryside.

Fantasies are often set in real places, ones that writers have revisited over and over, and which immediately trigger an erotic response. There are generic places (dungeons, dark alleys, bar washrooms, manors, hotel rooms and yes, even bedrooms), but some are also geographic locations that, over time, have been constructed as erotic, some kinkier than others. The Castro. How many encounters have occurred in the Castro? That's where Carol Queen's Femme meets her Leather Daddy, and also where lots of gay male porn is set. More generally, the city of San Francisco, named an "erotic city" by Josh Sided in his book *Erotic City: Sexual Revolutions and the Making of Modern San Francisco*, is intrinsically linked to many stories written by Patrick (formerly Pat) Califia and by the Samois group. And speaking of Samois, the group took its name from that of a lesbian dominatrix's estate in *Story of O*, again a significant place. For that matter, can any seasoned pornographer pass by Roissy anymore and not think of Pauline Réage's novel? Other big cities have a sensual charge: Paris, and its Pigalle district depicted in so many porn stories; New York, with memories of Laura Antoniou's fictional slave auctions and the penthouse apartment of John Preston's Mr. Benson; Tokyo and its manga-style erotic imagery, complete with elaborate shibari.

But Toronto? What kind of kinky images pop up into your mind when you think of Toronto? Okay, maybe memories of a special bedroom or private dungeon, but from a broader point of view, what kind of literary imagery? What is Toronto famous for in books, films, art? Are there streets, districts that immediately evoke warm bodies thrusting into each other, the scents of engorged sexual parts, the sounds of moans, screams, whip cracks and paddles meeting sweaty flesh? Do you remember a single hot scene that you read about in a novel or short story that was set in Toronto? Toronto has a baroque castle in its centre, a cock-shaped monument and one of the finest zoos in North America. So why doesn't it feel as sexy as San Francisco, New York, or Tokyo?

Toronto is a sexy, kinky city to live in and to visit. Plenty of kinky folks make their homes here – I could have filled these pages with a directory of names and the colours they flag. The city plays host to hot and well-attended leather events too, with the annual Toronto Leather Pride rendez-vous as a centrepiece. But, so far, its presence in the realm of fiction has been demure at best.

Soooo, enough complaining. Let's repair this error of literary history! Let's kink up the city of Toronto, wrap it in leather, and associate it with the kinkiest of stories. Let's put Toronto on the map of sexy fiction.

That's what I said to myself when I began plotting this anthology. I wanted us to contribute to the collective body of kinky sexual imagery by adding our own Torontonian flavour. They say that if you want something done well, it's best to do it yourself, so I solicited leather-loving writers of all persuasions to please come up with kinky stories about Toronto – which they did generously and enthusiastically. This anthology contains the best examples of their erotic imaginings set in the Big Smoke. The tribulations of adventurous tourists in the Church-Wellesley Village... dangerous strolls in the Don Valley... girl meets butch on the Yonge-University-Spadina subway line... risky blowjobs in the Harbour... heavy breathing on the Gardiner... rough abductions near Liberty Village... unexpected encounters in the Distillery District... dark desires in Leslieville... wet whippings in Queen West... Secret or not-so-secret play parties everywhere. And all these intense stories occur behind Toronto's famous diversity of tightly closed doors.

These Toronto places are the canvases on which the city's kinky stories are painted, and the settings lend each story a special colour and texture. Take a look!

The University Line

Andrea Zanin

When I asked her to write a bio and tell me why she decided to submit a short story for the anthology, here is what she sent to me: "Andrea Zanin likes to write stories about sex. And leather. And leathersex. And dykes. And leatherdykesex. Also cities, where leatherdykesex happens. She's clearly better at writing about the sexual fantasies of the urban leatherdyke than she is at writing bios. No, her story isn't a true story. Mostly. Yet. Anyway. She'd like to thank the Academy, and God, and — what? Oh. Um. Did you know that cows are the world's leading producer of methane? Andrea needs more sleep. She thinks this anthology is a unique contribution to Canadian leather/dyke/etc. culture and is very happy that her work is nestled into these pages alongside that of such a grand collection of fabulous pervy writers. If all these stories got naked and fucked in a giant orgy of paper and ink, what do you think they'd spawn? Just curious. Find Andrea at @sexgeekAZ on Twitter and at sexgeek.wordpress.com."

No need to add more. I think this is sufficient ground to make one want to lick someone's boots.

Sometimes I picture the city criss-crossed by millions upon millions of colourful footprints, each of us leaving a distinct trail, a constantly evolving map. Where do the colours run so thick they bleed together? Where do two tracks stop, and then change directions in lockstep? Where are all the places where paths almost cross, for years at a time, but not quite — a few steps too short, a few moments too early? Sidewalks and line-ups, streetcar tracks and bicycle trails, the worn places on the subway staircases. These are all places that bear the weight of our lives, that carry our lines. Urban animal tracks, habit and whim, commute and exploration.

The first time I noticed her, it's because her pants were too short. That odd habit that some slightly older butches have, of wearing trousers that end just above the ankle, with hiking boots or the like. They couldn't be bothered with style — and yet they have one, and it doesn't include dresses. After assessing the hem situation, I glanced up from my seat on the subway and noticed a slight academic stoop, black-rimmed spectacles, short salt-and-pepper hair due for a cut, crow's feet, a firm jaw. She was intent on her book, so I opened mine and entertained myself, between paragraphs, looking over and noting small details. Compact hands, strong and practical. A sporty nylon shoulder bag. By the time the subway let us off at the terminal, I'd pegged her as one of my kind. No, I mean a scholar.

Despite being employed by the same sprawling suburban Toronto university, or at least so I assumed, we didn't encounter one another again for many months. Orange trail meets green trail, randomly, one day in a blizzard. Or almost. You gotta love public transit for its furtive observation opportunities. This time, a tall gangly man and a short, well-bundled one waved down the 196B just as it was pulling out. The driver kindly stopped, doubtless taking pity on them in the driving snow, a rarity for Toronto these days. The pair boarded and squeezed in next to me between the wheel well and the driver's box. I was deep in thought, gazing out the window into the snowy night and doing my best to ignore the various cell phone conversations going on around me. My feet were sore from a day of teaching, for which I persistently wear high-heeled boots even though I always end up suffering by the time I'm heading home. After a few minutes, though, I realized that I was picking a line out of the hum of voices around me, a sort of mid-range tone, very cultured. I think it was when I caught the words "exceptionally thought-provoking" that I realized, all in one go, that the short guy wasn't a guy, that she was the professor I'd spotted last year, and that good lord, I could listen to her talk for hours.

I flicked my gaze up to the window to catch her reflection. Yup. Indeed, freed from the confines of a blue tuque and heavily bundled scarf, her face glistened with the melt of a few stray snowflakes, and her cheekbones caught the unflattering neon light at just the right angle. I couldn't turn around, so I was left to listen in to her entire conversation with her gangly colleague. Department politics, deadlines, the arbitrary nature of the academic status machine. All this awaits me when I finish this damn PhD, I thought to myself. In the meantime, I can put it off as others' concerns. Her words weren't really the point, though. Her voice, now, that was worth riding on for a while.

The bus emptied us out of its belly at Downsview station, and the line of passengers trickled deep down into the earth, colourfully tiled walls making the escalator descent a cheerful one. I noticed that she and her colleague stayed within a few feet of me on the platform. Deliberately, or by coincidence? We headed into separate doors when the subway arrived. Green and orange trails split, but remained on a parallel line. The creaking, battered train smelled like piss, as it often does. I pulled out my book and tried to read. The words wouldn't quite work, the lines overlapped.

Wilson, Yorkdale, Lawrence West. The snow filled the air outside the windows between stops. Glencairn, Eglinton West. Back underground now. As

I hefted my bag onto my shoulder when we reached my stop, I heard her voice again, this time saying goodbye to the gangly professor down at the opposite end of the car. My area of town is heavily populated by grad students and professors because it's the part of Toronto that's closest to the University line, which leads directly north. So it wasn't exactly surprising that she might live here, but then why hadn't I seen her around more? At the grocery store, the movie rental place, the bank? I bet she's a morning person to my night owl. Probably she loves Italian food while I prefer sushi. Green line and orange line, crossing in space but not in time.

I exited and headed to the staircase. Her small, denim-clad ass danced about eight inches from my nose beneath her down jacket as we ascended single-file while people rushed down past us to catch the train before the doors pinged shut. I felt oddly like I was invading her privacy, so I slowed down, but not before noticing that her jeans seemed brand new, a pair of dark-washed Levis, and not too short this time. Perhaps she was going home to her wife, who'd finally convinced her to ditch the old pair. Strong legs, I thought. Maybe a runner? Okay, *stop*.

Last leg of the trip. She stood directly in front of me as we waited for the streetcar, the bright red behemoth that would carry us each back to hearth and home. If I wanted to say anything, now would be the time. "Nasty weather we're having, eh?" Surely I could do better than that. "I couldn't help but overhear…" Nah, I wasn't interested in talking shop, or in looking like a stalker.

I examined the breadth of her shoulders. She squared them, glanced around. A flicker of eye contact. Then she turned her back again, pulled a smartphone out of her pocket, and got lost in social media. There, I thought. That is my answer. Perhaps she is shy; perhaps she hasn't noticed me; perhaps she just isn't interested. Regardless, I need a little more participation if I am going to cruise someone.

The streetcar clanged up to the stop, the crush of passengers pressed in, and I found myself standing directly next to the seat she'd managed to grab. Nowhere else to go. I wrapped an arm around the support pole, and wondered if she could smell the wet leather of my jacket, so close was her face. The anonymous intimacy of urban transportation had struck again.

She looked up, caught my eye. Shit, she knew I'd been watching. I felt a blush creep up my neck, but fortunately her crow's feet were crinkling — that had to be a good sign, right?

Her hand snaked out, touched the hem of my coat. That voice. "I like your jacket," it said. "The leather is beautiful." Orange line and green line finally met, asymptotes no more. There was a spark, like the electricity that crackles in the air overhead when the streetcar prong switches power lines.

The rest... the rest was easy. Like the way you walk with confidence when you're heading to work every day, because you know every step and turn, practiced movement along a familiar trail. "Seems to me I saw you on the subway late last year." "Yes, I just moved to the area last fall." "Certainly, I'd love to join you for tea." "It's late, though, the shops will be closed. Can I offer...?" "Yes, that would be lovely." It was like we'd been doing this for years. Green and orange footsteps tracing a tandem trail, off the streetcar, heels and boots striding side by side up the road. I slipped a bit in the snow. She caught my elbow. We laughed at the cliché. "What do you teach?" "Yes, that's definitely the best place for fresh produce." The door opened and we kicked snow off our boots before stepping inside. She took my coat, took my hand. I took a chance, took her mouth. She tasted of cold air and fresh apples.

When I fucked her, she lost her words. She had shucked off her jeans and I wouldn't let her fold them neatly. "Drop them on the floor and come here." Laid her down, explored her body, caressed small sagging breasts and strong deltoids, flat stomach and widening hips, pubic hair that wasn't in fashion but was wonderfully soft under my palm. My two fingers slipped inside deep, mouth closed hard against her nipple and hand tangled in her short curls to hold her just where I wanted her. Words gone, yes, all those multisyllabic tools of the trade abandoned, but that voice never stopped, moaning and sobbing and then yes, there was a *yes*, a clear loud "yes," and her body pulled hard and held fast and her letting go made me liquid inside. She tried to do that lesbian thing, where you take turns, but I couldn't let her touch me, not yet, too soon, no I don't want to talk about it, not now. I fended off her hands, let her come down, waited 'til her breathing slowed some, then pressed right back in. "I am not done with you yet. You aren't finished taking me in. Say yes again." And she did. So wet. Hot and slippery, not like snow, nothing like snow, more like the spring rising, a simmering vat of sap about to boil into thick sweet syrup. Four fingers this time, and I promise you next time there will be five and she will shout that *yes*, and yes, I promise you there will be a next time.

I left her in sheets soaked with her own come, breathing deep and slow, spectacles slightly askew. Folded her jeans and placed them on her dresser. I slipped out the front door, walked the three blocks home with slickness on my thighs, masturbated as soon as I got in the door, with the smell of her cunt still on my fingers. Footsteps alone in the snow, this time. Green trail practically glowing in the dark behind me. But now I know the way.

NOW!

Xris Morgan

My first memories of meeting Xris are at the Black Eagle in Toronto, where her strong, peaceful presence came across.

Xris Morgan has been involved in the Toronto leather scene for twenty-plus years, starting out in the punk scene and the Urban Primitive movement before finding the BDSM/fetish scene. She greatly values her leather family. Their closeness and support has been vital in helping her through many life transitions. She approaches play with a sense of humour and with a seasoned respect for boundaries and safety.

As a switch she can enjoy both sides of the kinky realm and lately leans towards blood sports and knife play, but she loves adventure so co-topping or group scenes are always welcome.

I hope you will enjoy reading her story "NOW" as much as I did. I like when the big city becomes a space when the most perverted desires can grab you at any instant.

❝Now!" the driver yells and the van door slides open and the three of us jump out. The target is directly beside the van, perfectly timed. She barely has time to gasp and I see the half-moons of fear in her eyes only for a second before a heavy cloth bag is covering her head and muffling the ensuing screams.

We grab her, bind her with zip ties, and pick her up still in that moment of shock, and dive back into the van with her in under five seconds, just as we had practiced. The door slides shut and the van peels out, tires screeching into the night. A few lights come on in the neighboring houses and a few dogs bark in protest but the momentary disturbance is quickly forgotten. Darkness and silence re-envelop the absence that has occurred in the back alleyway of this quiet, unassuming suburban neighborhood, washing away the evidence of what just transpired by returning its normalcy.

Zip ties work fast. They are cheap, come in many sizes, are readily available at hardware stores and at a great co-op store I know up north. Problem is that they can damage nerves and cause permanent damage quickly, so once the target is in the van, duct tape is used to bind her securely over her clothing. She is rolled and pinned like a protesting rag doll on the cold metal floor of the rented white panel van. Cotton ropes then bind her wrists and ankles. Once she is properly in place for long-term bondage, her wrists are secured to a metal D-ring on the cargo van floor and the zip ties are snipped off.

Now the fun can start. The bag over her head is not tied, the bottom is open to allow for air flow but the material is a double thick velvet, the kind used for theatre curtains, so she can't see but she can hear relatively well. We're not worried if she gets it off, we're all disguised anyway. I'm wearing a half clown mask, the other a cat mask and the third is wearing the *V for Vendetta* mask.

I reach into my bag and pull out the bandage cutters and begin the task of removing her clothing. She struggles so deliciously, the Cat and V laugh and secure her in place while I prepare to snip, snip, snip away her modesty. I start by removing her high-heeled shoes and throwing them across the van. They make loud clangs as they hit the metal sides. Then I cut away her nylons because I can feel how vulnerable it makes her to be in bare feet. Shoes are important to her, they symbolize power and now they are gone. I'm surprised at how tender and tiny her feet are. Her toes look like plump little worms with red hats. Then I begin to snip her pants and she begins furiously fighting and cursing and mixing in guttural noises of rage. She sounds like a trapped animal that is not yet convinced that escape is not an option.

The Cat makes comments about the futility of her situation and lets her know that we are almost out of the city limits while V pins her shoulders to the floor of the van. Snip, snip, snip, rip, rip, and rip. I'm enjoying unwrapping this sexy squirming gift of flesh, ripping off her designer suit all pinstriped, pressed, and dry-clean only. Prada I think it was.

Then the very soft cream-coloured silk blouse. I snip the buttons off one by one, flinging them across the van and they make a "ting" sound as they ricochet off the sides. Then on to her lovely bra… such a shame… I don't have to snip this, it's all black and lacy and undoes in the front but I do anyway. She's furious and shrieks obscenities at me for doing it. She sensed my hesitation while I admired her tight round breasts so wonderfully displayed for me in their expensive little packages but unfortunately the packages had to go. I pull the pieces of clothing free from her body, fling them aside and take in the view. So pretty. Her skin looks immaculate. Her nipples are so yummy, my mouth waters. I run a gloved hand over her skin and a new torrent of protest erupts from her body along with more guttural grunting.

Next is her underwear, a matching set, no doubt a sister to the bra I just destroyed. V takes claim to the panties and wants them as a souvenir. I agree and snip them, slide them free and hand the warm, damp, lacy ball to V who slips it under the mask to smell them. Inhaling deeply, V comments that she even smells rich. We all laugh and she squirms and tries to pull herself into a ball. I pinch a nipple and she coils up pulling her knees to her chest. I allow this and signal for them to ease their grip. She thinks she's accomplished something and immediately pulls her knees tight to her chest. I signal for them to roll her and they do, they grab her and roll her onto her knees. Her wrists are still bound securely to the D-ring in the floor, so now her bare ass is in the air.

What a lovely sexy ass it is, too. We all decide to explore her lovely ass. She's freaking out now having realized that she has potentially placed herself in a more vulnerable position. She tries to roll but the Cat is now sitting on her upper back and shoulders so she can't move. I caress her perfect ass cheeks and slide my gloved hand between the folds of her cunt, exploring. She hunkers down and pulls her knees in tight.

I reach in and grab her by her bound ankles and pull her knees out, securing her ankles to another D-ring on the floor behind us. V hands me a spreader bar which I attach just above each knee and tie the bar to the D-ring at her ankles.

There, now her ass is perfectly on display. I take my time playing with her asshole while she shrieks with frustration. It's all pink and perky and then I bite into those peach halves. She bucks and roars in response to the pain. I'm not biting too hard, just hard enough. I'm really enjoying her lovely ass cheeks. I pull them apart and bury the clown face in her ass and cunt. I knead them and I slap them as hard as I can. She squeals and tries to fight and I slap the other side too leaving red welting handprints on her creamy skin. I have to then lick these with pride. My gloved hand now continues to probe her cunt; she's very wet and swollen. I don't need any lube. Her cunt seems to suck my fingers in. She continues to buck in protest but eventually the movements become rhythmic in time with me fucking her cunt with my fingers from behind.

Then V takes position behind her wearing a cock. V enters her from behind, slowly sliding the full length of the cock into her. I continue playing with her clit from the side. The bucking is now humping. Once V is fully inside her V stops and waits. She squirms and feigns protest but she's not going anywhere. Then slowly she starts pushing back and grinding into the cock. V laughs and says she wants more and V starts slowly thrusting in and out to match her rhythm. But when she wants to speed up, V stops and says, "You will come when I want you to come," and the dance begins. Whenever she begins to thrust, V stops but I continue working her clit. She's going crazy after a while, then V nods and we both stop. V waits a few seconds and starts up at a good pace still telling her she's not allowed to come then smacks her hard on both ass cheeks at once. V tells her not to come but it's too late she gushes giant puddles all over the van floor and starts screaming. The driver turns up the volume on the stereo to mask the sounds emanating from inside the van, and accelerates. V smacks her ass cheeks again hard along with a deep thrust and another gusher happens. She's screaming now so loud that the driver turns up the stereo volume in the van again and I can hear the driver laughing.

Two hours to the cabin in the woods, that's where the fun will really start. Once the package is delivered, their job is done but they can stick around and watch.

The One in the Centre

Bliss

Bliss is a queer switch who has been active in the scene in southwestern Ontario for about seven years. She has co-presented on rope at Playground 2012 and for the So You Want to Be Kinky workshop series. As co-founder, she has been the administrative engine behind the GTA Rope Social since its inception in 2009, and also co-facilitates the Triple s Discussion Group, a monthly peer support and discussion group for slaves, submissives, switches, bottoms, puppies and other non-Dominant types. A regular attendee at An Unholy Harvest, she credits that amazing and supportive environment for encouraging her experimentation and growth as a pervert.

I think I knew of Bliss before actually meeting her, thanks to the Triple s Discussion Group. Or maybe it was at leatherdyke play party. Anyway, I remember meeting a quiet and serious person, and then gradually realizing I had met a fun and clever person too. I enjoy the diversity of conversations one can have with her, on topics ranging from feminism to science fiction, from kink to creative writing.

She did not say much about her story, but what I can say is that I enjoyed reading it because of the solid perspective it provides on an abduction scene. And also because it was hot.

"What am I doing here?"

The phrase kept running through my mind at regular intervals as I paced down Fraser Avenue in the twilight. My combat-style fet boots shone dully in the yellowed phosphorescent light that fell from the streetlamps far above my head. I could feel the silky lining of my new leather trench, bought just for tonight, slide across my bare skin with every step. I was wearing nothing except the trench, my boots and some thigh-high fishnets. The sensation was surreal. But then, so was this whole scenario.

I flinched inwardly as another alleyway loomed to my left, as I passed a row of industrial buildings. I quickened my pace just a bit, feeling vulnerable as the cool fall air crept up inside my coat and brushed past my cunt. I'd had to force myself to remember, as I left my car in the Green P parking lot up the street, that the club-hopping vanillas had no idea how little I was wearing underneath my coat. I had kept my eyes down and walked quickly past them, afraid that one look at my burning cheeks would give me away.

"What am I doing here?"

I reminded myself that I'd been dreaming about this for years. To experience being completely overwhelmed... to test the limits of my endurance... but mostly, I wanted to be the one in the centre. I'd watched many group scenes at parties over the years with an envious thirst. Three or four or more players focus their intensity on one deliciously helpless bottom until they are completely undone. Then everyone collapses in a laughing, groaning, sexy heap. From my outsider's perspective, it seemed like an incredibly bonding experience. For once, I wanted to feel like I belonged, in a way that spoke of tribe and trust.

My directions had been clear. Pay for overnight parking. Walk alone on Fraser Avenue. Look for a white van (why is it always a *white* van?). And a code word, so I would know the right folks were snatching me. That thought made me both laugh and shudder at the same time.

I made it all the way down the street without being accosted, body tensing every time a vehicle approached from behind. But they all passed me by. No vans of any colour. I reached the end of the street, where a chain link fence separated Fraser from a small gully filled with brush and garbage. Just beyond I could see the Gardiner Expressway, cars rushing past, the people in them oblivious to my fear, my excitement, my growing sense of ridiculousness.

As I stared unseeing at the traffic, I deliberated. Should I wait here? Walk back up the street? What if someone noticed me pacing up and down? Would they call the cops? The thought of answering the probing questions of some bland-faced cop spurred me to action, and I spun on my heel and headed back up the street. If they hadn't snatched me by the time I reached Liberty Avenue, I was going to get in my car and leave. The last of my nerve was about to run out.

Decision made, I marched straight ahead, no longer darting furtive looks into alleyways as I passed. Of course, that's when they grabbed me, emerging swiftly and quietly from the lip of the second alley. A hood went over my head and strong arms pinned mine behind my back, dragging me into the alley. Despite all the emails, the careful negotiations, the late-night fantasizing, my instincts kicked in. I struggled frantically. My hindbrain was convinced this was real and I was fighting for my life.

Then lips pressed up closely against my ear, giving the code word in a calm, firm voice. I stopped struggling. I'd asked for this. Literally begged for it, at times. But now that the moment was at hand, would I really be able to give up this much control? While I pondered, they bundled me into the back of the van.

I could see nothing, but I could feel a soft mat underneath me. I smiled at the thoughtfulness, but any smugness was soon swept away. My wrists were quickly secured in leather cuffs and clipped to a hard point. As the van roared to life, hands tore open my coat and roamed my body, caressing, pinching, squeezing, slapping, and lightly punching.

Hands reached up underneath the hood and started wrapping something around my head, across my eyes. A separate piece was wound over the lower half of my face, covering my mouth. As wrap after wrap stretched and bound my face, I thought, "Vet wrap!" The world became muffled and I entered a state of submissive silence, unable to speak, my cries and moans silenced beneath layers of clingy fabric. My cunt gushed a little.

The van drove carefully, but still I felt tossed about on corners and when the driver had to brake. I was afraid of getting nauseous, but all those hands kept me distracted. So many hands! Were there three or four pairs? I couldn't count, they moved so quickly, darting along my body sensually, demanding and reassuring, teasing and arousing. Next came lips and teeth, kissing, sucking and nipping everywhere. No inch of my skin went untouched or unexplored. The attention crescendoed to an overwhelming sensory merry-go-round and I began to panic, thrashing against my restraints, the moisture of my heated cries condensing against the vet wrap sealing my mouth.

Suddenly, everything stopped. I panted into the silence. My skin cooled a little, the throbbing in my head subsided. Then one slick cunt began to slide along my shin. I moaned, my need surging again as the cunt ground against my leg. I tried to push further into the wetness, but hands held me fast, unable to move as the cunt humped my leg. Soon other body parts joined the fray. Cocks slapped against my thighs, tongues lapped my tits and belly, hair brushed against hypersensitive skin. I undulated against my restraints in a wanton display of lust.

I lost track of time. The van braked suddenly and we all slid forward, tangled together. I heard a distant rumble, and the van inched forward slowly, then came to a final stop. Body parts, hands, and warmth slowly began to relinquish my body. I heard another clattering, louder this time, and then felt a rush of cool air as the back door of the van opened. My bound hands were unsnapped from the hard point and separated, my coat completely removed. Multiple sets of hands tugged me down toward the door and lifted me effortlessly into the air, a rare experience for most adults. The weightlessness created simultaneous flashes of fear and wonder, and then I was being strapped naked onto a gurney.

I could feel myself being wheeled up a ramp, then through a series of twists and turns. Still blindfolded, with my hearing muffled by the wraps around my head, I could only sense the surroundings through my skin – a rush of cooler air, the vibration of machinery, the thundering of the gurney wheels over a grate.

Suddenly the air was cozy warm, and I was being lifted efficiently by several pairs of hands onto something large, solid and padded. My wrist cuffs were each secured to a top corner, and cuffs were added to my ankles and tugged apart. When I tested my restraints, I could not move my outstretched arms very much, but my legs felt the coolness of chains and they had almost a free range of motion.

A half-hood was snugged over the top of my head, covering my eyes and ears. The vet wrap was removed from around the lower half of my face, and my head was lifted, a bottle of water pressed to my lips. I sipped gratefully.

I faintly heard retreating steps, the squeak of the gurney wheels, and then... nothing.

After the constant barrage of touching, lifting and positioning, being left alone felt even more vulnerable than being under the control of so many hands. I shifted on the platform, trying to determine its contours with my body. I learned nothing new. I tried to shrug the hood off my head by twisting against the platform, and then my shoulder, but it didn't budge. I guessed it was made of latex or rubber.

I wished for something to cover my nakedness. I wondered what would happen when I had to pee. I thought about everything that had happened in the van and felt my own wetness leaking onto my upper thighs. I felt the sticky juices of others drying on my shin. I kicked my feet and rattled my chains. Nothing happened. Time dragged on. I fell into a light trance and drifted away into a dream state of tongues and hands and teeth.

Suddenly, I was slapped awake. Or rather, my breasts were. Startled, I gasped, even though at first, the slaps were relatively light. First one breast, then the other. Outsides, then insides. Rhythmic, deliberate, firm, the slaps gradually became more harsh. My flesh began to heat, then burn. My nipples were not spared, nor my especially sensitive areolas. Slapping turned to light punching, then something hard and smooth, like a paddle was turned on them mercilessly. My aroused moans turned to cries of pain, then tears. Still the blows rained down, with barely a pause between them. No words were spoken.

As suddenly as they had begun, the blows stopped. I was left alone again, in silence, to feel the burn and itch of my skin as it absorbed and processed the pain. My clit throbbed. I groaned. Time dragged again.

How long before the footsteps returned? Fifteen minutes? Thirty? An hour? I could not tell. This time, my thighs were the subject of their concentrated percussion. Tap, tap, taps gave way to slap, slap, slaps and then punches, interspersed with the thud of a flogger, the sting of a single-tail bite, the bruise of a heavy paddle. Still, no words from my tormentor.

Finally, my wrists were unsnapped and I was given another sip of water, before I was turned over and re-secured. They left me to feel my painful thighs, the residual ache of my breasts, pressed into the platform.

Another what-might-be-an-hour alone in the dark and silence. I shivered, but not from cold. From intensity, from the physical and mental rollercoaster, from not knowing what would come next, how long this ordeal would last, or whether I would be up to the task. I began to rattle my chains, at first in frustration, then to see if it would bring someone. No one came. Later, I moved them just to feel something, anything.

I fell into a light dream state again. Suddenly I was alerted awake by the vibrations of someone approaching. There was no ramping this time, only the searing pain of cane strokes on my ass and the backs of my thighs. Hot stripes of fire, evenly paced and deliberate. I screamed. I begged for mercy. The whip-like strokes of the cane changed to annoying tap-tap-taps on acidic skin, unrelenting, over and over until I wanted to take that cane and shove it up their ass. I squirmed violently, I swore, I bucked. No answer. The tap-tap-tapping increased in speed and severity, until the pain cascaded over me in overlapping waves. I gave up and went limp, letting it wash over me. Then I flew.

Someone lifted my head, so gently that I whimpered, to give me more sips of water. I whimpered louder as I felt them leave again.

Even as I sniveled, a part of my brain admired this methodical, well-planned assault on my psyche. Someone was using my abandonment issues against me, and I both loved and hated them for it.

My arms ached. Pressure was building in my bladder, but I pushed it away. I didn't want to contemplate what the answer would be if I asked to go. My skin burned in so many places, I couldn't tell where one sore patch ended and another began. And there had not yet been one instance of penetration, not even my mouth. The realization made me sag into the platform in exhaustion. That meant we were a fucking long way from being done.

I fell asleep this time, for how long I don't know. Time stretched and then suddenly snapped.

I awoke to a swirl of movement around me. I could hear chains rattling, wheels squeaking, and the scraping of large objects. I could sense more people in the room, through air currents, vibrations and excited, muffled murmurs.

My arms were let loose, and I moaned as I tried to move them. I was deftly turned on my back, and warm, oiled hands expertly smoothed my arm muscles into moving order. Many hands stroked warm oil into the rest of my body, from neck to toes, soothing sore spots and awakening others. I moaned softly, nipples stiffening as my body responded to their touch.

Then my legs were opened wide and lifted, the chains rattling as my bottom half was elevated into the air. I thought I'd felt vulnerable before! My wrist cuffs were reattached to the side of the platform.

I felt a small stream of warmish water directed at my cunt. I smiled faintly, thinking they wanted to clean up my copious juices. But after I felt my labia thoroughly cleansed, the water continued, increasing in volume and intensity. The stream swept up and down my lips, focussing briefly on my clit hood, and then continued. Each time it swept upwards, the water would linger longer and longer on my clit, the delicious warm pressure building an answering pressure of my own.

Suddenly, I flashed on a memory of us sitting around one night, sharing masturbation stories. I remembered admitting that many of my early orgasms in puberty were brought on by warm, rushing water from the bathtub spout. I'd lie on my back in the tub, legs up on the wall on either side of the taps, and let the sensual waves flow over my cunt until I came, swiftly and powerfully. Later, I found there was even a fetish name for it on FetLife, "clit washing." I perved over pictures of elaborate bondage structures and big showerheads. Ah, I loved it when they used my admissions against me.

Just then, the stream of water narrowed and intensified, concentrating on my clit, and I started to come. Powerful orgasms shook my entire body, one after the other, each sounding a deeper note than the last.

They started to speak, then, finally. Words of encouragement... "There you go, baby... Yes, she's starting now... Come on, grrrl...." and triumphant whoops at each climax. The force on my clit relented briefly after each come, but it didn't stop, and it slowly dawned on me, through the haze of bliss, that another one of my dreaded wishes was about to be realized.

They would continue to make me come until I broke.

That's when the penetration started. A finger, then two, slipped into my cunt. Water splashed across my belly as the invading hand diverted water. Strong fingers stroked my inside walls, calling out my G spot as they called my name, called me dirty names. I broke out in goose bumps, as a thin sweat covered my entire body.

Fingers retreated, only to be followed by something smooth and cold, with regular bumps that continued to tease my G-spot mercilessly. I recognized the familiar feel of my favourite glass dildo. How the hell did they get hold of that? Confident hands pumped the dildo slowly at first, to give my perennially tight cunt time to accommodate the stretching, and then faster as my juices began to flow.

"That's it, baby girl, take it all for us."

"Fuck, yeah!"

"Come on cunt, open up!"

On and on they fucked, and miraculously, my cunt opened to receive them. The intensity built and then built some more, my head tossed side to side as my G-spot screamed for release. Suddenly I gushed, not knowing how much of the flood pouring out from between my thighs was come or piss, and not really caring one whit.

I had gulped no more than half a dozen breaths when the showerhead returned in full force. I screamed as another orgasm, painful this time, ripped from my body.

Something popped into my ass, deliciously painful and stretching. The glass dildo remained stuffed inside me. A cock slid skillfully into my throat, and I hit that place where ultimate submission brings internal orgasms, shocks that cause my body to undulate uncontrollably.

I thrashed on the table, mindlessly and wantonly, as each of my holes was stretched and fucked. They swapped out the showerhead for a strong vibrator on my clit. I tapped out, indicating I needed the cock to be removed.

"I hope that vibe is… uh, waterproof," I grunted.

"Oh, still able to make jokes, are you? Crank that vibe!" And someone did, at the same time that strong fingers cranked my nipples into tight twists.

My inner beast emerged, growling at the back of my throat, as more orgasms continued to rollercoaster into each other, alternately sending me flying around the room, or crashing me back into my body with painful accuracy. They yelled, cajoled, roared and hooted. I begged for mercy.

"What's your phrase?" My lips set into a determined line. Did I mention I was also stubborn? "Well, ok, then!"

The orgasms lost all pleasure, became all pain. I cried. I sobbed. I shrieked.

"What's your fucking phrase, cunt?"

I drew a shuddered breath. Everything stopped. Oh, the humiliation.

I whispered.

"What's that? We can't hear you. Speak up!"

I mumbled a bit louder.

"Not good enough, sunshine. All right, let's give 'er! Harder!"

They started in on me again, and I screamed, "Bananas in my pajamas! Bananas in my pajamas!"

Now that it was out, I babbled the humiliating phrase over and over, not caring about the helpless laughter that tumbled about me, just wanting the torture to finally stop.

That's the last thing I remember for a while. When I woke up, I was clean and dry, swaddled in something soft, and in the middle of the most deliriously happy puppy pile I'd ever experienced.

Someone was giggling, someone was coming loudly, and two were fucking... but most importantly for me, I was being patted, stroked, kissed and cuddled to my heart's content. Later, I knew I would feel all the sore bits, but for now, I was adrift in bliss, amazed and proud that I had endured.

"Welcome to the tribe, sunshine."

Torontophilia

Artists: Virilia Crush and Mée Rose
(a Femme Handshake collaboration)

Virilia Crush: Lover, creatrix, sacred intimate and worker in Toronto. "Conceived and raised in Toronto, I am still in love with this city, with a hard-on for the CN Tower. Oh my Free-Standing Temptress! You are skewer, sceptre, axle, common ground, weapon and wand – orienting us home."

Mée Rose: A queer feminist artist living and working in Toronto, Ontario. "In my practice, I explore various mediums such as photography, video making, writing, and music. Over the past decade, my photography has been almost exclusively about the creation of erotic self-portraits, but I am now opening up to projects working with subjects outside of myself. I took particular interest in working with Virilia Crush to create "Torontophilia" as a way to experience another person's love for Toronto as different from my own. There was a technical challenge not only to frame Virilia alongside the tower within a shot, but also to capture her perversion and express it adequately enough. It is true that we, as Torontonians, all connect with this architectural centerpiece in our own way, but maybe the success of "Torontophilia" can be measured by how we've inspired folks to re-imagine the sexy possibilities!"

(Editor's note: Someone did it, Virilia Crush and Mée Rose did it, and I am delighted that someone did.)

Buddies

Eeyore Thudonkey

Joanne, a.k.a. ThuDonkey, is a smart ass. Her primary kink is intelligence, and she'll follow you home at the drop of a well-used four-syllable word. A sweet bottom whose butchness can apparently be seen from space, this donkey falls hard for clever femmes with short hair and glasses.

I got to know her at various kinky events, and I enjoyed her sense of humour and her even temperament.

Her short story "Buddies" is amazing because of the perspective it provides on the loved and desired one, and also because of the presence of a hot story within a hot story. Two stories for the price of one!

*S*he is brave. She does things that i'd never consider trying, goes boldly where i would cower in fear. Most nights i go home early and alone, knowing she will arrive later, full of the scents and sounds of an adventure. Yet i am not excluded; she will then curl up around me and whisper the tale for my ears.

The first time we went to Buddies in Bad Times, i was on overload. We had a hotel nearby, and had spent the day as tourists, taking in the streets of Toronto. The streets were different that night: darker, with corners occupied by all manner of queer pleasure, and brighter with the laughter and joy of queers celebrating and sharing their lives and bodies.

That mix of dark and bright followed us into Buddies, spilling out onto the dance floor and the quieter corridors still studded with a delicious blend of genders and sexualities and kinks being expressed. The combination was heady, but soon enough overwhelmed me, sending me back to the hotel.

She remained. And when her adventure found my ear, tucked under the covers, the images remained.

She said:

There was a lot of energy at Buddies, wasn't there? All the hyperactive gay boys with glow bracelets mixed in with the preppy lesbians; the leather dykes who picked Buddies over the Black Eagle mingling with the pin-up femmes; the wide-eyed first-timers side by side with the tattooed, pierced genderqueers. I had so much to choose from.

In the crowd I spotted someone I used to know: all in black, a PVC corset over a short leather skirt, fuck-me boots and a don't-fuck-with-me attitude. When I walked over to say hi, I got a first look at what she had at the end of the leash in her hand. She had a lovely boi kneeling at her feet, stripped to a tank top and boxer briefs and trying to look inconspicuous. The boi was skinny and gangly, and her hair was bristle-short and a dirty blonde. Her back was tattooed with an abstract mix of colours, but her ears were unpierced. Even before I saw her face, she was hot.

My friend recognized me as well, and we passed a few minutes catching up over the body of her boi before something else caught her eye. When she looked back at me, she was grinning.

"I've just spotted Dave and his boy. I really must chat with them. Would you hold on to this for a while?" She handed me the leash. When her boi started in discomfort, she added, "Feel free to use her as you choose. Her safeword is my name." With that, she strode off.

Imagine, *my brave one whispered to me*, there I was, suddenly holding on to a cute toy like that. Of course, I had to take advantage of this serendipity.

I ordered her to look at me, and when her green eyes hesitantly met mine I had her reiterate her safeword. Her voice wavered a bit, but she was clearly mentally present. That was all the encouragement I needed.

I stepped away from the wall and tugged at her leash to see if she'd follow. She did, crawling after me on the sticky floor. I kept a measured pace, but made sure to also keep enough tension on her collar to direct her. I ordered her to her feet for the stairs, and led her down to the basement. Fortunately there was a convenient corner as yet unoccupied.

I braced myself in the corner and tugged her collar to get her positioned between my feet. It's lucky I was wearing my skirt, isn't it? *My brave one led my hand to touch her thigh under the skirt, but stopped me there.*

I guided her head up underneath my skirt, and hooked fingers under her collar to control her movements. The boi caught on quickly, and nuzzled high between my legs, eager to please. I kept her there for a while, moving against my knickers as I watched other folks watch us. It was quiet enough that she could hear me when I told her that everyone was watching, that everyone could see her ass in the air and her face buried in my pussy. I could feel her breathing speed up at that thought.

Eventually I got bored of the tease and pulled her to her feet. I grabbed her crotch to see whether her cock was secured well enough for her to fuck me. It was. I fished the condom out of my bra and told her to suit up. She snapped to the task with alacrity.

When she was ready for action, I tugged my knickers aside enough, and guided her in. That brought her head close enough to me that I could whisper, "You don't come."

Her "Yes, Ma'am" felt even better than her cock.

I grabbed her ass to control the fuck completely. You know I like it that way. *i nodded as she continued the story.* I worked her in and out of me until I was close to coming and she was panting like it was torture for her not to come. Then I pushed her out of me and to her knees in one movement. I pulled her face in close to my pussy again, so that she could see me as I worked myself to an orgasm.

When I finished, she was still on her knees in front of me, dick hanging out, panting. Mmm.

I had her tuck herself back in, and tucked the condom away. I led the boi back upstairs, and grabbed a beer to wait for my friend.

My brave one brushed her hand over my hair as she finished her story. She had me panting and wet, as always with her adventures, and i purred slightly under her hand.

"Do you think you can sleep now that you've had your bedtime story?" she asked, and i nodded under her hand. Soon i heard her breathing shift pattern, and when she was asleep i was able to rest too, knowing the adventure had brought us both home.

Leaving

Elizabeth Lister

I included the following story because of the insight it provides into lifelong desires and the challenges of fulfilling them as one ages.

Elizabeth Lister is a stay-at-home mom who enjoys writing down her vivid and explicit male/male fantasies. She published her first two novellas, *Exposure* and *The Crush*, with MLR Press in 2011. She published her first full-length novel, a graphic BDSM M/M erotic romance called *Beyond the Edge*, with MLR Press in 2012.

Beyond the Edge was nominated for the ILA-International Writing Award 2012 and the Goodreads BDSM Group Members' Choice Awards for 2012. It was a featured read for the month of April 2013 in the BDSM on Goodreads group and was recently designated a Recommended Read by Kinky Book Reviews. Her story here features the characters of Freddy and Patrice from *The Cross and the Trinity*, sequel to *Beyond the Edge* and currently a work in progress.

Elizabeth's writing has been described as "sensual and thoroughly seductive" (*Top2Bottom Reviews*, 2011). Her stories feature graphic sex scenes that sometimes "qualify as literary orgasms" (*MM Good Book Reviews*, 2011).

Elizabeth can be found online at
- www.elizabethlister.ca
- moderneroticromance.blogspot.ca
- www.facebook.com/ModernEroticRomance.

You can purchase her books at www.mlrbooks.com or Amazon.ca.

❝My name is Frederick," the young man murmured in my ear as I sipped my scotch, enjoying the burn in the back of my throat as much as I enjoyed the feel of the boy's hot breath on my ear. "and I need a place to stay tonight."

I cleared my throat. "You can stay with me. But I'm not going to touch you. You're far too young."

He laughed, an uninhibited sound that warmed my heart even as it ridiculed my words. "Whatever you say, old man."

††††

I drove him through the cold, slushy streets to my condo in Toronto's Distillery District. On the way I learned he was originally from Ottawa and currently enrolled in the undergraduate Sociology program at the University of Toronto. He needed a place to crash because his roommate had his girlfriend over for the night.

I'd recently sold the condo in favour of a historic home in Montreal and my place was in the process of being packed up, since I would move in just one week. The fashionable nightlife of the French city seemed more to my taste these days, although the hustle and bustle of Toronto had suited me for a long time. In my younger years, the incredible diversity and the sheer size of Ontario's capital had been a powerful draw. It was the closest thing to New York City that Canada could boast.

I greeted the concierge as we entered the lobby and noticed his skeptical glance at Frederick.

"My nephew," I said with a cool smile, although why I felt I had to explain myself to this man was a mystery.

Frederick took my hand in his while we waited for the elevator, lacing our fingers and transmitting welcome warmth to my cold skin. When the elevator doors opened, he pulled me into the small space, regarding me with a teasing smile. I noticed he had the sweetest dimple on one side and the greenest eyes I'd ever seen.

"Your nephew, huh?"

I shrugged.

He laughed again. I found myself smiling, genuinely this time.

The elevator stopped at my floor and we exited into the hall. The bright overhead light made him appear even younger than he had in the bar. I'm sure I looked older. I keyed us into #1405.

He gazed curiously at the cardboard boxes and lack of furniture as we entered the unit.

"Moving in?"

"Out, rather. In a week," I said.

"Oh."

"To Montreal."

"Why?"

I shrugged. "It's where I grew up. I have family and friends there."

"I've never been."

"The bedroom," I said, walking ahead of him through the wide, industrial space, "is not quite as deconstructed."

He followed me to the large room at the back of the unit. The antique bed frame, dresser and armoire looked strange in the modern space. They would be the last things to go.

He removed his jacket, laying it on the wing chair in the corner. I took mine off as well and laid it on top of his. He walked over to the large window and gazed upon the lit expanse of downtown Toronto.

"Wow! Great view."

Looking at the handsome young man framed in the dark window of my bedroom, I had to agree. But I said nothing.

He moved away from the window and sat on the bed, running his hands over the luxurious coverlet, gazing with excited eyes at me. Leaning back on his slim arms and kicking off his army boots, he patted the bedspread beside him.

I hesitated.

"Come on, old man. We both know you didn't bring me here to play checkers." His green eyes burned with energy and mischief.

"Would you like a drink, Frederick? Are you old enough to drink?" I said, knowing that would annoy him.

He laughed. "Yeah, I'm old enough. But just."

"You're *nineteen*?"

Jesus Christ.

"I'm twenty. Not that it really makes a difference."

I felt a wave of relief because it did make a difference to me, although I'm not sure why. At least he wasn't a teenager.

I went to the kitchen and filled two juice glasses with some Pinot Noir I'd had chilling. I'd packed the wine glasses, of course.

When I turned around, there he was, standing right in front of me. He took one of the glasses from me, drinking the wine in several languid gulps, holding my gaze. In my peripheral vision his Adam's apple bobbed sensuously beneath his skin. When he'd finished, he handed the empty glass back to me, wiping his lips with the back of his hand.

"Guess I was thirsty," he said.

"Guess you were," I replied. "More?"

"Sure," he grinned. "But you don't have to get me drunk, y'know."

I smiled as I followed him back into the bedroom. "I'm not trying to get you drunk, Frederick."

"Call me Freddy."

"Do I have to?"

"Yes."

Jesus.

My dick had been hard since he'd whispered in my ear at the bar. Now it throbbed. Did this beautiful boy really want me, or was he after something else?

"Look, if it's money you want, I'll lend you some. I won't pay for sex. I'm not that desperate."

"You think I'm trying to hustle you?"

"I don't know. I'm wondering why you're here."

He shook his head, looking down at the floor, and then up at me. "I want you." I stared at him, trying to determine if he was sincere.

He sighed and shook his head. "Look, I just want something *real*, y'know? An experience. Something to... treasure." He looked up from under his lashes at me. "You look like you could deliver it."

I took another drink of wine, not sure what he meant, but knowing the things my body wanted were very real.

"You seem like you know who you are, if that makes any sense. Maybe you can help me figure out who *I* am, who I want to be. How old are you anyway?" he said, peeling off his shirt and throwing it onto the floor by the closet.

"My name is Patrice and I'm fifty-one," I managed to say, taking in his finely formed torso with its pink nipples and dusting of brown hair.

"That's about what I thought."

"So 'old man' is somewhat of an exaggeration."

"Sure. Anyway, you look great, Patrice. For someone your age." He smiled. "I've always had a thing for older guys."

He started peeling off his jeans.

"Wait a moment," I said, even though I could hardly wait to see him naked.

"Why?" he asked.

I placed the glasses on the dresser and walked over to the light switch. "This room, it's too bright."

He watched me curiously as he took off his jeans and threw them on top of his t-shirt, then peeled off his boxer briefs. He stood there, young and unashamed of his own beauty.

Remember those days, old man? "Don't you want to see me?" he said, and I felt the last bit of my reluctance drain away.

"Of course I want to see you, Freddy. It's you seeing me I'm worried about."

He made a face. "I want to see you. I wouldn't be here if I didn't." He reached over and pulled the cord on one of the small bedside lamps. "Let's keep this on, okay?"

I nodded, flicking the main switch, so that the room became bathed in the soft red glow from the lamp. Freddy got up onto the bed and lay back against the pillows, holding his erect penis in one hand and angling it toward me.

The excitement built inside me at the prospect of bedding this handsome boy, now that I'd finally given myself permission to do so. And once I'd admitted my desires, I couldn't help laying everything on the table. Perhaps he'd run, and maybe that would be best anyway.

I turned, opening the drawer nearest me. I didn't need to be able to see in order to gather what I needed. When I had everything, I approached the bed and the circle of light, holding my hands out before me.

When Freddy saw what I had he muttered "Fuck," and sat up straighter. His eyes flew to meet mine, his forehead creased in worry.

"Only if you want to," I said. "I like it. Maybe you will too."

"You want to tie me up?" he said quietly, his eyes flitting back to the soft black rope in my right hand.

"Oh, Freddy. I don't even need to fuck you, beautiful boy. I just want to play with you for a while." I cleared my throat. "Maybe spank you?"

"Dirty old fuck," he said, and I felt the shame creep up. I didn't often feel shame, but looking at this very young man, it came upon me. I saw myself as I must appear to him – desperate, weird, old.

"You can leave if you want," I said, my confidence shattered.

He took the rope from me then, running its softness over his hands, and stared, fascinated, at the large steel plug, still in its packaging, that I held in my left hand. Then he stretched out, letting the rope fall onto his pale, youthful skin like a thick, black spider web.

"I'm yours, old man," he said in that sultry tone, "or should I call you 'Daddy'?"

The pleasure surged inside me, no shame anymore.

I nodded. "Yes."

"Okay. Tie me up, Daddy. I've been a bad, bad boy..."

"Are you sure?" I asked, so wanting to do this but still the responsible older man.

He laughed. "Patrice, I can already tell you wouldn't hurt a goddamn fly. Well, at least, not any more than it wanted it."

I grinned and nodded. "I don't want to hurt you, Freddy. At least, not very much."

He sighed and I think I saw him tremble. "Oh fuck. Let's stop talking about it. Just do it. I'll tell you if I don't like anything."

"Promise?" I said.

"Yeah."

†††

Trussed up on the bed, spread-eagled and bound by my expert knots to the four corners of the frame, Freddy looked like something out of a bondage magazine feature. He was perfect. So young and fit, his skin flawless and smooth – unmarred by age, tattoos or piercings. Beautiful.

The big steel plug nestled inside him now, pushing on his prostate the way it was meant to, teasing me with its presence and the fact that I'd put it there. His thick cock curved in a long arch over his flat belly, a tempting pearl of dew at its tip, taunting with its glistening essence. I wanted to lick it off. I wanted to swallow that cock and make Freddy come. I wanted to hear him scream with pleasure.

But not yet.

First I had to worship him. It seemed like my duty as the older, kinky man, to kiss this lovely boy all over, giving him the joy of that tenderness and softness before I spanked the living shit out of him. At least, that was the plan.

I took my time enjoying the softness of his skin, the purity of his scent, the hoarseness of his moans and grunts as I touched and teased him with an experienced man's finesse. Perhaps he'd never been with someone who knew what they were doing. Maybe that's why he'd come with me, why he wanted me.

"Oh, yes!" he moaned as my fingers teased the glans of his cock, dancing there and down the length of his shaft, rubbing so slightly. He panted desperately, pulling in his bonds, trying to get more friction while the hard steel massaged him from within.

"Is this what you came for?" I asked breathlessly, my own cock hard and aching at the sight of him this way. "Is this what you wanted, Freddy? Is this real enough?"

"Yes! Fuck." He moaned again.

"You're a very naughty boy, Freddy," I said calmly. "For wanting this."

He nodded. "I know. I know." He looked up at me with yearning, craving eyes.

"I'm afraid I'm going to have to spank you."

He jerked at those words, thrusting his cock up into the air, letting me know how much he wanted it.

"I'll have to untie you."

"Oh fuck yes…"

I untied his wrists and ankles, slowly, although I was as eager as he. When I'd released him I stood him up by the wall.

"Lean against the wall and put your hands behind you."

I tied his wrists together at the small of his back, bending his elbows slightly. "Keep them up here. I want your bottom exposed. For obvious reasons."

He nodded. I felt his arousal and anticipation as if they were my own. He watched me as I returned to the same drawer, this time taking out a wide black leather strap. When I struck it against my palm, he jumped.

"Do you want it?" I asked, making sure he understood and would consent to this game. There would be no ambiguity tonight.

"Yes, Daddy..." He murmured hoarsely, pushing his ass out at me, practically begging for it.

Running a trembling hand over that sweet bottom, I located the base of the steel plug and nudged it back and forth, before getting down to business. Leaning my head against the wall beside him, staring into those guileless green eyes, I moved my hand in an effortlessness born of years of practice.

The impact of the leather connecting with his innocent flesh made a satisfying thwack. He gasped a hissing intake of breath and closed his eyes for a moment. When he opened them, they gleamed.

I hit him again.

We breathed hard and loud. His cock surged and dripped, he was so aroused. I knew the plug made the experience even richer, because each time I struck him, it pushed inside while the muscle clenched around it, giving him intense pleasure even as the burn from the strap assaulted him.

"More," he pleaded. His brown hair lay damp against his forehead, his cheeks blushed red, his eyes shone bright and alive.

My mouth dropped open as I gave it to him over and over. I watched his reactions, listened to his moans and whimpers, being extremely careful with the force of the blows.

Finally, after about ten hard strikes, he said, "I want to come now. Please."

A statement and a request uttered with such grace and faith that I immediately dropped the strap and grabbed his chin, kissing him fiercely. He pushed his soft tongue into my mouth, moaning gently and letting me suck at him desperately. I forced myself to pull away because I could have continued for a very long time.

"Of course," I said breathlessly. "You've been such a good boy."

My left hand went to the base of the steel plug while my right hand slid down his smooth chest, pinching a nipple as it passed, and then wrapped around his desperate cock.

"You look beautiful," I said, my own breaths coming quicker from watching him. "I want to see you come."

He nodded, shutting his lovely eyes as I stroked him and rocked the plug gently.

"Oh... fffuck... oh... God... oh... yeah... faster... faster... oh... oh..." he gasped until, with a yell, he came, squirting white seed onto the grey paint of my bedroom wall as I watched, wide-eyed and reverent.

"Oh yes," I murmured repeatedly, until he finished and sank to his knees.

I knelt beside him, petting him as though he were a precious animal in my care. Truly, I wanted him. After only three wonderful hours I wanted him for my own, when I would probably never see him after this night.

"Are you all right?" I asked.

He nodded. "Are *you?*"

"I'm wonderful. Thank you." I untied his wrists and threw the rope aside.

He shook his head and pushed himself up. "Come here, old man," he said, taking my hand and leading me over to the bed.

We lay down together. Looking into my eyes he took my erection in his hand and stroked me until I came hard, trembling, moaning and clutching his warm shoulder.

"Freddy," I said gently when I'd recovered. "You should really see Montreal."

He smiled. "Sure."

"Will you come and visit me? After I move?" Suddenly, Toronto seemed like the last place I wanted to leave.

He laughed. "Of course I will. I'm sure I'll want another spanking. That was a good one you just gave me."

"I know," I said. "It was. You were very brave."

He kissed me softly. "G'night, Patrice."

"Good night, Frederick."

We fell asleep together above the lights of the city in the echoing, almost-empty condo.

†††

In the morning I bought him brunch at Café Uno. He marvelled at the chic industrial space while loading his plate with cheese, smoked salmon, croissants and scrambled eggs.

I sipped my latte, enjoying his unselfconscious gluttony – the product of a youthful metabolism and eventful night. I tried to memorize the way his skin glowed in the morning light and how his eyes shone with remembered passion whenever he looked at me. I'd given him my business card with more personal contact information scrawled in ink, but who knew if I'd ever see him again?

"I guess I should have fed you last night."

He grinned at me while shovelling more scrambled eggs into his pretty mouth. "I always eat a big breakfast."

"What are your plans today?"

He swallowed, wiping his lips with his napkin. "Well, I have to go home and do some laundry, then I'm meeting my friend Sarah to go shopping. How about you?"

I sighed, playing with a piece of croissant. "More packing, I suppose." Part of me wanted to ask him to spend the day with me, but he had plans and I had work to do.

When we'd finished our meal I paid the bill. We stood and put on our coats.

Freddy leaned in and kissed me on the cheek. "Thanks, Daddio," he said, "for being real." And he was gone, the chimes on the door announcing his exit.

I adjusted my scarf, and blinked back the tears that had suddenly appeared in my eyes. *Sentimental old man*, I berated myself silently. It would never have worked anyway.

Need Fire

Allison Armstrong

Allison Armstrong is a polyamorous, femme-dyke domme. She lives with her wife in Ottawa, Canada, where she writes erotica, runs the Voices of Venus women's poetry showcase, and gardens whenever possible. Her work has appeared in *Bywords Quarterly*, *Venus in Scorpio*, *Hyacinth Noir*, and *The Floating Bridge Review*.

The first time I met Allison must have been at An Unholy Harvest, a few editions ago. I was impressed by this fierce, tall woman, by the pretty objects she made, and later, after getting to know her better, by her serenity and her beautiful voice.

About "Need Fire," she says: "I chose to submit this piece to *Leather Heights, Toronto, Canada* because there are dykes whose bodies don't get enough air-play in lesbian smut, and I think that needs to change; and because I wanted to show an overtly spiritual side to the power and intimacy inherent in that which we do."

Her long, lean body is covered in scars, each one revealed to me as her robe slips from her shoulders to puddle on the floor. Some of those scars I know only in passing — familiar as neighbours, but no more than that — the thousand nicks and cuts that come to pass over a lifetime of camping and climbing, hiking up and down the Rockies. Some of them I know far more intimately. Some of them I made.

Tamar Freya, my mountain girl. A daughter of the oil patch, she fled east even as I was pulling away from my Nova Scotia roots, skipping Halifax altogether, and heading for Church Street, where I thought I might find my tribe. I like to say that I met her halfway, but the fact of the matter is that I met her in Toronto; met her at the Cameron, nearly a decade ago.

A lot of water has made its sluggish way down the Don since then.

When I met her, she was as newly out as I was, and her body was a blossoming mystery, unknown territory that I had to learn, inch by inch, as we learned each other, slowly, over tea in her basement apartment and over praise and wine at monthly Sumbels, through ordeal rituals at fests and retreats and in the back rooms of women-only play parties. Then, her black hair was short, barely past her jaw and growing out of a shaggy bob, a cluster of daisies tattooed at the small of her back, and recent scars still bright against her forearms. Now, her hair has grown long, braided into a thick, dark rope that falls over her shoulder. Now, we share a home on Silkweed Lane, our threshold marked with *Algiz, Inguz, Othila,* a crabapple – its red fruit wizened in the cold – growing by our door.

The moon is full tonight, casting its light through our window, bright on the snow that has heaped itself on Toronto. The four posts of our antique canopy bed are wrapped in protective loops of dark hemp. Leather cuffs dangle from them, ready for use, but we don't need them tonight. Tonight is not a night for knives or razors, not a night for ropes or leather. Tonight is a night for bodies, hers and mine, in adoration. Around us, candles flicker on every surface, heating the room 'til we have no need for clothes or blankets. I shed my own robe, let the satin fall to the floor. Naked, she stands before me and, naked, I circle her, tracing my fingers along the small of her back. I brush them across the thick, white scar just above her waist, the souvenir of a fall while climbing; and down the elaborate tattoo, newly completed, that follows the column of her spine – a tall, slender birch, its crown circled by the full moon, *Fehu* and *Manaaz* entwined with the cluster of daisies at its roots. Pausing behind her, I brush my hands over her arms, before turning her to me. I cup her face in my hands, press my body to hers as I lean in to kiss her mouth, her brow, her throat.

"Mine," I murmur, shifting to twine my fingers in her hair, to hook them in the worn leather of her collar.

"Yours," she answers. "Always yours."

I trace my fingers lightly over the pale, faded scars that line her arms – the marks where, she confessed to me one night, she'd sliced into herself at twenty-three, sinking razor into flesh in order to focus, to give herself an explanation for why living had to hurt so much.

I lift her hand, run my tongue over her forearm, sink my teeth into her wrist and hear the inward hiss of breath as her body tenses. She breathes out, slowly, a sigh of pleasure, body relaxing, and I kiss my way further up her arm. I tease the hollow of her elbow with my tongue, then kiss, nip, slurp my way up to her shoulder. Here, there are scars I know well. They are fine, small, even delicate, and there are five of them, one for each finger that I dug into her shoulder the night she fisted me at an out-of-town party, the night I rasped *harder, harder,* into her ear while her strong, skilled hands dove into me and my nails ripped deeper into her back with every thrust.

Now I sink my teeth into the place where my forefinger and thumb once left their mark, leaving the imprint of incisors and eyeteeth in her flesh, and it is she who groans *harder, harder*, into my ear as I bite and bite again, savouring the salt taste of her skin on my tongue.

Nuzzling her neck, I can feel her pulse against my lips, my open mouth. I could linger here for hours. Another evening, I might, but tonight I am impatient, nipping lightly at her earlobe before moving down, down, over the worn leather of her collar, the delicate curve of her clavicle, across the expanse of her breast bone where faint white lines show the word I've scratched and cut – *Beautiful* – backwards, so many times, so she could read it in the mirror every day.

I push her, not gently, onto the bed and she stumbles, falling without a word, her arms open, spreading herself before me. Call it communion. I worship her body by devouring her flesh; tracing my tongue up the inside of one thigh and down the other, grazing the sensitive skin with my teeth, promising pain to come and reveling in the way she shudders and jumps under my mouth. Crawling between her legs, I nuzzle her mons, trail my tongue along the orchid petals of her labia as she sighs, her clit waking and lifting in response. Slowly, I work my way up her body, nibbling her hips, tracing the circle of her navel, grazing the delicate curve of her rib cage, her sternum, until I find her breasts.

Sucking and slurping, I wash her nipples with my tongue until I taste milk, until she is arching her back and gasping, her clit rigid between us. I want to bite her, sink my teeth into the tender spots on the undersides of her breasts, tear at her nipples so hard that I taste blood. But not yet. For all that I'm impatient, I still want to hear her beg, and I know I can outlast her.

I press my thigh between her legs, giving her something to arch and push against as I scrape my teeth across the warm curve of her left breast, circle her tight nipple with my tongue. I slide my free hand up and over her ribs. If I look, I know I'll see the cluster of dark red lines that mark where I pierced her, two years ago, dragging each of the pink- and green-tipped needles out of her so that she was left with a spiraling red rosette on her right side. My fingers twist, digging into her ribs, leaving purple bruises over remembered red. She yelps, short and sharp, and drags breath back into her lungs.

"Hurt me," she gasps. "Please."

"What was that?" I drag my nails across her breast, just hard enough to tease, and she groans.

"Hurt me."

I slide my tongue across her nipple, graze it lightly with my teeth, and she shudders.

"Say it again," I tell her. "Ask for what you want."

"I want you to hurt me."

I grin against the swell of her breast, then lift my head and, stretching, place a gentle kiss on her lips.

"Remember," I remind her, "You asked for this."

She grins at me, her smile alight with anticipation, and I can't help but grin back before diving between her breasts again. This time, there is no tenderness, no soft, teasing touch of tongue or fingertips. Instead, I snap and bite, quick and light, all over her, leaving a mass of livid red welts in my wake, making her breath come in short, sharp, gasps. This isn't fun for her – she likes the slow, deep pain that grows and blooms into pleasure. She's doing this, accepting this, for me. And I adore her for it, how she whimpers and yelps in it, as she whimpers and yelps. I bite the sensitive places under her arms, along the line where her bra band sits, where the underwire will rub all day while she's at work. I want to leave her marked so she'll remember.

Finally, I take her fiercely, slowly, the way she likes it. I sink my teeth into her hard enough, deep enough, to hear the almost-crunch of crushing flesh. I know there will be dark bruises there before morning. She cries out, struggling under me, but I use the weight of my body to hold her down, pinning her wrists with my hands, and grinding my hips into hers, refusing to let go. Slowly, her cries melt into moans, and her struggles take on a new rhythm. I unclench my teeth, run my tongue over the deep impression that they have left, and she shivers, her hips moving against mine. When I bite down, hard, again, she doesn't whimper but only hisses, a brief in-draw of breath, before sighing, all the tension going out of her. I breathe with her as her breath deepens, let go her wrist to stroke her exposed nipple with light fingers even as I grind my teeth into her flesh. Her back arches under me, and her words come out in a whisper, *please, please...*

I know what she wants, what she always wants. Slowly, I relax my jaw, let my tongue slide over the deep teeth marks, tracing them, dropping kisses over the red welts that mar her skin. Between her breasts, there is a deep scar, keloids raised dark and permanent, shaping the rune *Berkana* where I have cut and re-cut it year after year. Now, I run my tongue over it, tracing each line of the rune, grazing it with my teeth. She pushes her hips against me, breathing deep and steady. This is the root of it, the deepest reason for our monthly ritual, calling my beloved back into her body through pain and pleasure entwined.

"Tell me your name," I instruct, and the syllables trip off her tongue while winter moonlight falls across her body and mine. She names herself and, at her naming, I bury my teeth in her scarred flesh, twist my sharp fingers into her bruised and tender breasts. She cries out, deep and guttural, her body shuddering under me.

Tamar Freya, I think, naming her again, silently. *My beloved.*

When her breath steadies, and her shaking calms, I press a kiss into her breastbone, and move to lie beside her.

"Mine," I murmur, wrapping her in my arms.

"Yours," she answers. "Always yours."

[Untitled]

Jack E.

Jack is a Two-Spirited queer academic, parent, activist, teacher, drag/neo-burlesque performer and, obviously, a kinkster. Not necessarily in that order. Formerly on the board of Montreal's Unholy Army of the Night, he can frequently be found engaged in acts of debauchery with other queers and gender-transgressors in the Montreal-Toronto-Ottawa corridor.

Did his story really happen? There was indeed a conference in Toronto, but not that year. And he did indeed perform a drag number at Goodhandy's, but it wasn't a strip. That strip number was indeed performed, but not outside *la belle province*. The scruffy academic who turned out to be a big, mean top, and all the depraved acts described in the story are, alas, fictional. But one can always hope. You can read some of Jack's non-pornographic writing at http://tboyjacky.wordpress.com.

The first time I met Jack, he was not aware that I was there, in the audience, watching him play, dance and strip on stage. Right then, I knew I wanted to know him. He has now become a friend. Being an academic myself, I am very happy to publish his story, which offers a sexy contrast between academic functions and the raunchiness of desire.

Ah, my first trip to Toronto. I remember it fondly. May 2007. Way back before I had top surgery. I'd already been on T for two years so I had a fine furry face and was past the squeaky-adolescent-male-voice phase. Perfect for cruising guys.

Of course, cruising guys wasn't the official reason for my visit. I was actually there for an academic conference at U of T. But hey, what kind of perv would I be if I didn't mix work and pleasure?

Being a drag performer back in Montreal — What? Did you really think I only mix work and pleasure when I travel? — I managed to get myself booked for a kinky genderfuck strip number at good ol' Goodhandy's nightclub on the Friday night of the conference weekend. The timing was right — they were having a drag night and the local troupe agreed to have an out-of-towner in their show. So along with my laptop, presentation notes and other nerdy delights, I packed my leathers, lingerie and, most importantly, my precious nipple clamps.

Now, I'd heard about some of the deliciousness that happens at Goodhandy's so it was quite difficult to fully immerse myself in the joys of academic discourse as I attended conference session after conference session on Friday, mixing with some of the top names in my field. Fortunately, my own presentation wouldn't take place until the next day, because I don't think I could've refrained from sliding in a series of titillating innuendo after titillating innuendo into my talk. Not that your average anthropologist would mind. But still.

†††

I arrived at Goodhandy's early that evening. I walked around to get the lay of the land until it was time to go backstage, change and psyche myself up to take it all off. Well, for the sake of accuracy: to take *most* of it off. In reality, what mattered the most in this act was that bit that stayed on...

When the show started, I waited for my turn with the usual pre-show jitters: that mixture of butterflies, sweaty palms and an inner voice that chants: "Don't worry, if anything goes wrong, just take your clothes off!" And then I heard the opening sounds of DaRude's "Sandstorm."

I swaggered on stage with an air of cocky confidence that I only really enjoy when I'm faking it. I exuded learned masculine energy as I strutted around in my leathers. After I threw away an unlit cigarette with a put-on macho thrust, the first thing to come off was the leather jacket. That hint of more to come off was enough to get a reaction. As I continued with my macho strutting, some of the people near the front — many of them dykes and genderqueers, the usual drag king audience – egged me on. With their looks and their gestures, they dared me to take more off. It was much fun and they were hot, but one guy that caught my eye as I postured – with his shoulder-length hair, scruffy beard, ripped-at-the-knee jeans and denim vest over a black leather jacket – just continued to lean against the wall on the side, looking rather indifferent. As if he'd seen this kind of thing before and was skeptical about my ability to surprise him. I wasn't worried.

Loud exclamations and hoots emerged near the front of the stage at about 1:35 in the song when I unzipped one leg of my chaps and invited a cute round femme to unzip the other. Knowing they were expecting a pair of hairy legs and knowing I would not disappoint them, but knowing that they would not be anticipating what was covering most of those hairy legs, I opened both legs of my chaps to reveal a set of sheer black thigh high stockings lined with pink.

To loud and surprised whoops from the front of the stage and to the widened eyes and tilted head of a certain denim-and-leather-clad – ahem – gentleman, I quickly removed my chaps, leather vest, black t-shirt and chest compressor to reveal a sexy black corset. Proceeding to prance around with feminine slink swankiness – also learned – I looked over at my mystery man from time to time until he reluctantly smiled and nodded his head slightly, as if acknowledging that the joke was on him.

At 2:58, when I made motions to unsnap the corset, taking my sweet time to do so to incredulous looks and howls of delight, I set myself up for the final surprise. Oh, not the boobs... by now, they must know that was coming. Even *that* guy. Then at 3:12, as I threw the corset into the air, exposing not just a pair of tits but a pair of nipple clamps linked by a chain, I knew I'd gone beyond his expectations. As I wiggled my tits around, making the chain move and catch the bar lights, I knew I had his interest... at least as a performer. For the rest, we'd see.

†††

At the bar, sipping on a ginger ale, I looked around for him. Wondering if he'd disappeared. Thinking that maybe he just wasn't into trans guys and gender fuckers. I valiantly flirted with others, of course, but I kept hoping. Something about him drew me, even though I hadn't spoken a word to him. Maybe it was because he reminded me a bit of the kind of guy I went out with in high school, when I was a rocker chick. Maybe that, combined with him being in a queer and kinky space, made me think that worlds could collide in surprising ways. Maybe it was just that uncontrollable physical reaction I have to scruff. That urge I get to sit on a scruffy guy's lap... rubbing my crotch on his, running my hands through his beard and neglected hair.

When I got up to wander around, I spotted him, leaning against a small, high table and looking around. And of course, just like in all the sappy stories, he chose that moment to look in my direction. And as our eyes met – yes, more sappiness – he smiled in recognition.

I walked toward him, somewhat apprehensively. He smiled and gestured toward the table, inviting me to join him. "I liked your act," he said in my ear, to be heard over the music.

"Thanks," I grinned. "I know some people like it but some people get a little... ummm... confused and intimidated by it."

"Well..." he trailed off, uncertainly. "I mean, it kinda threw me for a loop. I was expecting a straight-up drag number. The only surprise, at first, was that someone from the conference was here at all. Not that it should come as a surprise that there would be other kinky anthropologists around this weekend," he grinned back.

I laughed and cut myself off abruptly. I looked at him carefully, imagining him in regular academic garb. "Christ! I *do* remember you. We chatted during the coffee break! I remember thinking you'd be cute if..." It was my turn to trail off, embarrassed.

"...if I didn't look like a stuffy academic?" he asked with a sly smile. "Hey, I was only dressed that way because I was presenting. On days when I'm not, like tomorrow, I go with a more casual look. *Everyone* does that." Seeing me roll my eyes a little, he added: "Oh wait, I remember you saying you're presenting tomorrow. What should I expect? More of this?" he teased as he gestured toward my leather gear.

I could only look at him. I envisioned kink-filled nights with the tossing about of words like *hegemony*, *phenomenology* and *ontology* interspersed with rimming and fisting. He looked back intently and I could feel my clit and cunt lips swelling.

"Wanna get out of here?" he asked suddenly. "I think we could hear ourselves better at a café or a diner."

"Uhh, yeah sure. That would be great. I missed your talk, you could tell me about it."

Incredulously, he replied: "Yeah, that's right. We can talk shop if you *really* want."

My put-on cocky confidence gone, I just chuckled.

†††

As we headed down the stairs, he asked me where I'd like to go.

"I dunno. I don't really know what's around here, it's my first time in town." I turned on the bottom stair and looked up at him. "Maybe you should... lead the way."

He looked at me knowingly, then looked at my left hand on the railing. Seeing where his eyes went, I slowly turned my hand over on the railing, making the palm face up, open to him. "You asked for it, *boy*," he said gruffly as he grabbed my wrist tightly. Forcing me to turn back toward the exit, he let go of my wrist, grabbed me by the scruff of the neck and pushed me out the door.

Once outside, he tapped me on the left shoulder to signal where I should turn. After a few minutes of walking, during which I shook inside, wondering what he was going to do to me, he grabbed me around the waist and made me stop. Leaning over, he asked me if I really wanted this. I, in turn, asked him the same. "You know I'm not a typical guy... you saw what I am."

Turning me around and looking me up and down, he replied: "Yeah. I saw what you are. It's all new to me. And I won't say it doesn't confuse me. And I sure as hell haven't gone near pussy in a long time. But fuck, your energy... I just want to do fucking nasty things to you. It'll look different than what I'm used to but fuck that shit. I'm an anthropologist! I can handle unfamiliar territory." He smiled roughly at me.

I only had enough time to get out a half smile before his mouth turned into a strict, straight line and he told me to step out into the street and hail a cab. "Where are w—" I had time to get out before he grabbed me by my hair and told me to shut up. "You'll find out when we get there, *boy*," he spat. "Till then, shut the fuck up."

I obeyed, and a cab soon stopped for us. We got in, he gave directions and we were off. After about fifteen minutes, the taxi let us off near Queen's Park. I recognized it because I had come to eat my lunch there during the conference that day. I looked at him confusedly, wondering why we had come close to the university.

"I'm staying in a student's apartment that I sublet and I have it to myself," he told me. "But I thought we could take a little walk through the park first." Looking around slyly, he led me to the park. As we walked along the path, he grabbed my hair again and told me what he thought of me. "When I first saw you, I knew you were the type who needed to be put in his place. Looking all cheerful and smart in the daytime, cocky at night. I just knew you could use a bit of knocking around. Someone to come along and make you crawl a bit."

My throat was dry. My face was flushed and hot. My cunt was flooded. I looked down at the path in front of me and thought about putting one foot in front of the other.

He veered off the path, knowing I would follow. Near a tree, he stopped and ordered me to get on my knees. Trembling, I obeyed. Not knowing where to look, I glanced up at his malicious face. He slapped me and told me to look down until he told me otherwise. I could hear him muttering something about a stupid boy.

I heard him unzip his jeans and thought I would finally get to give the blow job I'd been craving for so long. The thought of a hard cock in my mouth gave me a little tremor throughout my body.

"Take off your jacket," he said. "That's right. Now put it aside. Faster, dummy. Take off the shirt now, hurry up. That thing — whatever it's called — take it off too." I pulled my binder off and put it with my jacket and my shirt.

Tits exposed to the warm May evening air, I felt my nipples get hard. "You're proud of those tits aren't you, showing them off like that. Well, I'll show you what I like to use my boys for — and those tits of yours will just add a little something special. Hold them up for me!" he said urgently.

With that, I felt his warm piss on my exposed tits. As if they weren't already as hard as they could be, my nipples got even harder. As if it wasn't already as wet as it could be, my cunt got wetter. Finished, he shook his cock over me to get rid of the last few drops. He zipped himself up. "Now lick your tits clean. I know you can reach. Then get dressed." I complied, lifting up each breast in turn and licked his piss off them. I quickly got dressed and waited for him to give me his next order.

"Get up already!" he spat at me. He walked away and I followed. We walked all the way to the apartment where he was staying a couple of blocks away. When we got in, he turned to me and slapped me again. "Now you're gonna get the real treatment. Take it all off, boy. Take it all off. Put it over there.

That's right. Now stand there. Back against the wall. Close your eyes."

I didn't wait very long before he started using my tits as punching bags. I gritted my teeth, my pride preventing me from crying out. He punched harder, making them swing with the force of his punches. I couldn't prevent groans, moans and eventually screams.

He stopped punching then and quickly grabbed my nipples. "Nipple clamps, huh?" he said in a mocking tone and with an equally mocking smile. Without waiting for a reaction, he twisted them with what I guessed was all his strength. Delicious pain rocked my world. I began to sag down. He let go of my nipples and grabbed each of my tits firmly with his hands. He swung me one way and then the next and finally tossed me toward the bed.

"Get on the bed and show me that boy cunt," he ordered. I obeyed and got on my back. Holding my legs open for him, I waited for the next ordeal. Minutes passed as he examined me, brushing fingers against my cunt lips and against my clit. Probing inside me with his fingers. Finally, with a "Jesus Christ, I forgot how wet a cunt could get," he thrust his hand inside my dripping cunt. He got on his knees on the bed, between my legs, put his free hand on my throat and proceeded to fist me painfully until I thought I would pass out.

"Ok, that's enough," he said finally. "I didn't bring you here for *your* pleasure, I brought you here to use you. In the bathroom. Get on the floor, on your knees, bitch."

Unzipping himself again, he followed me. Apparently, he had to piss again. "Open your mouth, you brat!" he hissed. I obeyed and soon tasted his salty piss. I glanced up at him as I devotedly drank him down, and saw his stern and angry face looking down at me. "That's it, I knew you were a fucking piss bucket." It didn't last as long this time. I licked my lips as he shook his cock above me once again. Seeing that I had closed my mouth, he slapped my face hard. "I didn't tell you to close it, you piece of trash," he said menacingly. I opened my mouth for him and he spat in it. "That's what I think of you. Now keep it open. Wide."

With his hand on the back of my head, he thrust my mouth onto his cock. I took it in my mouth and felt it harden. Finally. The cock I craved. In my mouth. I whined with pleasure and I ran my tongue around his growing erection. Pulling his head away from his fully hard cock, he slapped me. "You're doing this for *me*, not for *you!*" he barked, spitting on me again. Then he thrust himself into my mouth again and shoved hard, making me gag repeatedly. "I'd like to see you try to give a fancy talk now, trash. Come on, suck it!"

After several minutes of fucking my mouth, he pulled my head back. Spitting on me again, slapping my face and telling me I was useless for sucking cock, he made me get up and bend over the side of the tub.

"That's it. I'll see if I can make use of your ass, at least. That's one thing I'm used to. You'll have to stand up tomorrow to give your talk."

With both hands on the side of the tub, I waited. I sighed with pleasure and pain as his cock slid into my ass. Over and over again. I snuck my right hand between my legs and furiously rubbed my clit. When I came, I felt my ass tightening around his cock. Then he kept thrusting. The night was still young.

†††

I wasn't the only panelist who chose to stand to give their presentation at the conference the next day. Given the height of the desk where the computer was placed, it was much easier to use PowerPoint that way. That's my story and I'm sticking to it. No matter how hard he stares at me as I discuss my slides.

Fucking Toronto

Jacqueline St-Urbain

Jacqueline St-Urbain has been a shit-disturber on the Canadian leather scene for over a decade. The founder of the Unholy Army of the Night and the co-founder of An Unholy Harvest, Canada's annual weekend for leatherdykes, transfolk and ladyqueers, she is a hardcore switch and frequently a wicked and inventive sadist. Jacqueline has always had an unsettled and unsettling relationship with Toronto, though she'll admit there's some fine chocolate to be found in the city.

The first time I met Jacqueline was at An Unholy Harvest. I can't remember which happened first — seeing her beautiful corset or being hit by her beautiful, powerful singing voice. However, I fully remember when she hit me for the first time with a flogger — but that's another story.

The reason why I chose to publish her short story in this anthology will be obvious when you read it. I love how Toronto is present as an actual character, both as a bitch and as a desirable creature.

T

oronto is a bitch.

I lived in Toronto for a while — dark years — and we never warmed to each other. And it wasn't just me. Toronto is vicious and heartless; she'll lacerate you and leave you to bleed on the curb. She's New York's insecure little sister, big and self-important, but her puffed-up superior attitude is laced with whiny insecurity. Instead of knowing she's the biggest and baddest and best, she's always looking south and envying her sister-rival. It laces her uncaring with petty meanness.

If you met Toronto in a bar she'd be rake-thin and nervous, with bleached-blonde hair that should have been retouched and trimmed two weeks ago. She's wearing clothes that are two sizes too small. Glam trash. A small black leather mini that lets you catch a glimpse of her ass when she bends. It clings to her hips; you can see the bones through the second-skin skirt. Her flashy halter top is too tight and you can see her hard nipples catch the light as they change the way it bounces off the silver lamé. She's wearing cheap hooker heels with silver straps across her pink toes. She's a skittish, constant smoker, incessantly calculating the next time she can get out into the alleyway for a haul of nicotine. She smokes Gauloises unfiltered, and the ash floats from her twitchy fingers onto the pavement as her ragged nails flick the next tiny bit away.

But there's something about her. A brazen, lurid suggestiveness. You can't help but wonder what the appeal is, why she's had so many, why so many flock to her. And yet you feel it too, which is why you follow her from the grimy bar into the even grimier alley behind.

She doesn't even talk to you. She knows you've followed her out here. She looks at you through absurd fake eyelashes, taking your measure. Another drag on her cigarette, another look at you. You meet her empty eyes, then look away. She's got you where she wants you. The cigarette goes on so long you begin to wonder if she's smoking a fake – or is time just turning to treacle? You can't meet her eyes so you look at the slushy concrete of the alleyway, which is why you catch the downward fall of the butt into the oil-slick puddle.

So you have a second or two of warning before she grabs you by the hair and pulls you in for a kiss. She sticks her smoky tongue past your teeth and crushes you against her painted mouth. It's an impersonal invasion. You're just the nearest pair of lips.

Abruptly her ropy arms spin you around and press you into the brickwork of the building's backside. Her tits are pressed into your leather-clad back and her hands are running over your flanks like you're a horse she's thinking of riding. Since you are, it's an apt impression. You're learning the brickwork intimately with your cheek as she runs her tongue over the exposed back of your neck and you tremble in her arms.

Her hand slides its greasy way under your skirt and one finger finds your soaking panties. Her face is close enough to yours that you can feel the muscles pull into a smile as she growls, "Uh huh." Her voice is low, smoky and smug. You feel your cheeks redden with embarrassment that your arousal is so obvious. A rough finger slides into your cunt, which grips it in vain. She slips out again as quickly as she entered, and grabs your ass instead, squeezing enough that you whimper a bit. Her thin hips press yours into the wall as she scrapes her nails across your butt cheek, making you moan a bit more. In this position, your nipples are hard against the rough bricks, scraped each time she moves you slightly. You're starting to feel them burn.

Those wiry muscled arms turn you once more and you feel her hands on your shoulders, pressing you to your knees. You're so aroused and caught by her confident sadism that you sink quickly to the ground, ignoring the protests from your bare knees as they hit the gravel. The toe of her hooker shoe nudges your knees open, and your own skirt is short enough she can see your underwear. She hitches one scrawny leg up onto the wall, and from your vantage point you can clearly see she's not wearing any. Her clean-shaven cunt is neat, but you can smell her scent. It's overpowering in its earthy aroma, a bouquet of swamp and musk and sewer in July. She reaches one hand down to pull her lips apart, and your mouth opens in response. But it's not her cunt you taste; it's the acrid, hot spurt of her piss passing your lips and rushing down your throat. You sputter and close your eyes but keep your mouth open as the city's piss rushes down your throat and spills out of your mouth onto your shirt, your chin, your skirt. Even your knees feel slightly wet now. Will she never stop pissing on you?

Finally the rush turns to a trickle, and as you dare to breathe for the first time in what feels like minutes, she presses her piss-covered lips to your mouth. The expectation is clear, and your tongue seeks out her clit as she grinds her cunt into your face. She laces her fingers in your hair and angles your head against her labia for her satisfaction. You find a rhythm that seems to work, a frantic sucking of her prominent, hard clit that almost feels like you're giving her a blowjob. You can feel her sinewy thighs tense as she nears orgasm. Your neck hurts, your jaw starts to ache, but her hand keeps you at the right angle – the angle that will get her off. She's rocking now, working herself up on your face, using you like she uses everybody.

Suddenly she crushes you into her and you feel her jerk as she comes, once, hard against your lips. You suck feverishly, overwhelmed with the desire to please her, this fickle, ugly city. You only wish to be lost in her, to be accepted, to be taken into her good graces, to please her. The pain in your knees, the ache in your jaw, the piss on your face, none of this matters anymore.

She ends with a grunt and a shudder, and pushes away from you, releasing your hair and pushing off of the wall with her foot. She looks at you, sizing you up, then pulls out another cigarette. She lights it quickly, cupping the flame so that her made-up face is suddenly briefly bathed in orange light. She turns away and walks to the other end of the alleyway with her back to you. It is obvious you have been dismissed. Your clothes are wet and stink of piss, your knees hurt, your jaw is throbbing and your panties are soaked through.

She finishes her second smoke and heads back into the bar. You don't even get a second look. She won't even talk to you; don't try to start a conversation. She's chewed you up, and now it's your turn to be spat out. You had your minute with her, and now all that's left is her smell on your clothes and her taste on your lips. You'll live with the ache for years, that she used you and spent on you, but you weren't found worthy of more.

Toronto is a cruel bitch, but you went into it with your eyes open.

Don't say you weren't warned.

Tuesday

Jenn Jenkins

Jenn Jenkins is a creative little lion grown in New Brunswick and recently transplanted to Toronto. Yes, a lion. At least, this is how she describes herself and dresses for parties. And creative, she sure is: she blogs, she paints, she felts, she knits and, sometimes, she writes kinky stories. She says she loves passion, connection, chemistry, mutual energy, and brains – but skin is her favourite!

You will find all of this in her short story "Tuesday." What I liked in this story is the little voice that is constantly speaking, commenting, analyzing… until she cannot anymore. Maybe that is what Jenn means when she says that rituals and rules make her happy and, yet, being pushed outside of her comfort zone brings her reflective growth.

It was Tuesday. May loved Tuesdays despite their predictability. Or perhaps routine was the very thing that made her happy in an otherwise chaotic life. Either way, it was here again and she began envisioning the events of the upcoming evening as though they were stored on a disc in her head stuck on auto-play, while she chased the tiny TTC token down the sidewalk.

"Remember to mend the hole in your pocket when you get home tomorrow," she said out loud to herself while finally capturing the token.

May could remember when she first moved to the city. Leaving the family farm behind was bittersweet. She missed caring for the animals, and the loft in the barn had been home to many a fantasy and a few fondly remembered realities.

Having arrived in Toronto with barely more than the clothes on her back and what fit in a small duffel over her shoulder, May made good use of library Internet access to learn where queer-friendly events were taking place. Being homeless was something she could handle, but being alone terrified her.

She met Marta and Ophelia at a queer slow dance on Dovercourt. Her small Baptist-country town barely had a spot for dancing, period, let alone a place exclusively for anyone who didn't fit the common hetero standards. Never mind the fact that May had barely kissed a girl despite her undeniable attraction to them, let alone experienced anything remotely kinky. That's how she could best describe Marta and Ophelia: kinky.

Fourteen months after her arrival in Toronto, May was still seeing Marta and Ophelia once a week on Tuesdays, and proudly called them her owners. The simple silver heart-shaped dog tag she wore on an inexpensive chain around her neck was inscribed with "M + O's sweet little slut puppy." She never understood the slut puppy reference, but beamed whenever she touched it.

At first, their meetings were especially explosive as May was introduced to mind-blowing orgasms tangled in a dark web of tease, tickle, and torment. She kept a journal for her owners, and when they realized how overstimulated the Tuesday night sessions were making her, May was denied any self-pleasure.

It didn't matter much that many months later, each Tuesday night was a carbon copy of the previous one. May spent the previous six days craving a release from the heat between her legs. Every small detail of her Tuesday built on the desire within her. Even the simple ritual of dropping the coin in the subway station turnstile caused her clit to dance in anticipation, breaking her concentration and reminding her of the importance of her task to arrive on time.

With her head against a window, May closed her eyes and hit play on the video in her mind. She did it to herself every week. Every night, really. She enjoyed the challenge of not wiggling in her seat on the subway train while memories of weeks gone by played like a live show for a private audience. May sighed out loud and wished the rails were just bumpy enough to get her off.

She would arrive at Spadina station and then take the 510 as far south as it goes before meeting Marta in a parking garage. Marta worked nearby but she lived west of the city with Ophelia. The drive would be like every previous Tuesday. Marta would hand May a silk bag when she climbed into the backseat of the car, just after she buckled into the middle seat. They would exchange no words. The bag would hold a small vibrator. May would lift her skirt as Marta adjusted the mirror once they were in thick traffic on the Gardiner, being careful to ensure Marta would have the only view of her bare pussy.

Marta's phone timer would be set in advance to go off at two-minute intervals. When the bell dinged, May would obediently buzz her hungry clit with the small toy. On the next ding, she would stop. Alternating two minutes on and two minutes off and never permitted to come, May would fill the car with the scent of her desire, pleasing Marta very much. Ophelia would arrive home before them by six minutes. She would video chat the two commuters over their iPhones using FaceTime, breaking the silence and getting in on the last moments of the show just as May was nearly begging for release.

Oftentimes, May would break out in a sweat, and at all times she would be flushed, exhausted, and excited. Ophelia would meet them in the yard, a mug of tea in hand and a soft smile on her face that almost overshadowed the glint of anticipation in her eye. The two owners would take May by the hands, lead her inside, feed her something light, and after brief small talk about their day-to-day lives, they would move into the playroom.

As if on auto-play herself, May would undress shyly and Marta would pat the bondage table quietly, motioning to May to hop up. Ophelia would remove her dog-tag chain and replace it with a custom leather collar from Halfway Creations. A number of well-worn leather belts and straps would quickly bind her down tight. She could see the order of the belts in her mind. Even the process of being bound was ritualistic and never-changing. May loved feeling secure and held beneath the straps.

In the next two hours, May would be punched, slapped, flogged, and tickled, in that order. She hated being tickled, and her owners knew it. After being released from the bonds, she would turn over on her back and, without words, Big Red would make an appearance. May would suck the red dildo Ophelia had strapped on, getting it wet before her owner fucked her hard. Marta would mount her face while Big Red was being thrust deep inside of her very hungry pussy.

It would end in Marta gushing on her face, sometimes with May choking pretty severely on her owner's fluid, Ophelia pulling out before allowing May her own release, Ophelia being fisted by Marta on top of May, and finally the beloved Magic Wand finishing off a horny, lust-filled bottom. After a quick bite to eat, showers, and drinks, Ophelia and Marta would retire for the night with May at the foot of their bed.

May would wake first and cook breakfast naked. Ophelia loved it when the bacon grease snapped and sizzled on May's breasts. It just happened to work best for all three.

The woman's voice on the subway announced that the next stop was May's, so she snapped back to the present, oblivious to the subtle grinding in her seat that caused a few passengers to glace curiously at her. She gathered her things and headed to catch a streetcar.

The streetcar was always full and at this time on her Tuesday journey, May was ever aware of her flushed face and wet pussy. She often tried to think of anything but the hot time ahead as she couldn't imagine the Twitter scandal that a spontaneous orgasm on a streetcar would cause.

Traffic was on her side today, and in what seemed like no time, she was in the parking lot according to plan and repetition. Saying nothing to Marta, as was their custom, May climbed into the backseat, spread her legs and ensured that only Marta would be able to see her throbbing, wet pussy. She waited in silence for the silk pouch to be handed back to her.

Only, it never was.

Afraid to break her posture or speak out of turn, May continued to hold the hem of her skirt up. She wondered if maybe the vibrator was forgotten, or broken. She began to think she was somehow in trouble. She wanted so desperately to speak, but she was terrified. No, no, no, no, no! This is not the plan. This is not how Tuesday works. She held back tears, and when one finally escaped onto her cheek, she was terrified to move her hand to wipe it away.

This was not Tuesday. This was not her routine.

The phone rang, but this time it was a regular call instead of FaceTime. Marta didn't answer it on speaker phone and May was only able to hear Marta's one statement: "Expect us to be on time." She hung up, looked at May for the first time in the mirror briefly and drove on.

Before they turned into her owners' long driveway, a different silk pouch was tossed to the backseat. May pulled out... a blindfold. Instinctively she put it on without hesitation while everything within her was trembling.

Marta helped May out of the car, and led her into the house. Still no words were spoken, and May was gently pushed into a chair just inside the door where she waited for less than a minute before she heard Ophelia address her.

"Well there's our sweet little slut puppy." She tousled May's hair lightly, and fastened a bit gag around her head. Still in the front entrance, her clothes were removed for her and she felt four hands sensually caressing her body briefly. She felt safe, and loved, and very confused.

Her collar was replacing her chain. At least one thing felt familiar.

Or did it?

The sound of a leash clipping into the O-ring of her collar, followed by a quick tug downward that forced her to her knees – this was unfamiliar. A couple of quick, reassuring rubs on the ass were timed perfectly as the occasional touches were the one thing keeping May from experiencing an uncomfortable level of fear. She couldn't have been too uncomfortable, however. Ophelia remarked how insanely wet her sweet slut puppy appeared to be. May blushed hard beneath her blindfold and gag.

A belt was put around her waist. She thought it very odd. What she couldn't see, but later understood, was the pouch on the belt that held an iPod. Earbuds were placed in her ears, and she was led to a cage.

May had never been in a cage before. She had never actually been a puppy, despite often being referred to as one. Why the sudden change in Tuesday?

Her owners pushed play on the iPod before closing the cage door. May barely heard the lock snap shut before a familiar voice came on the iPod. The voice was Marta.

"Listen to me, sweet slut puppy," the recording began, "Tonight is a very different Tuesday." Her owner went on to tell her not to drift off, that she would have to listen closely for prompts and instructions among the playlist that was to follow. For now, she was to wait patiently on her hands and knees and then the music began to play.

She wondered, while listening to her owners' favourite swing music, what they were doing while she waited. The music was loud enough that she felt the intentional sensory deprivation and smiled. Tickled and terrified at a change to Tuesday, May was hornier than she had ever known. She could smell her own sex heating in the cage.

She hadn't heard the cage door open but soon became aware of a bowl of water between her hands. Right on cue, the music ended and Marta's voice returned, instructing her to remove the gag, but not the blindfold, and to drink all of what was placed before her. She lapped at the water as music continued. No matter how much she drank, the bowl remained full. It seemed likely that the water was being replenished, but she stayed true to her task.

Eventually, after she found the bottom of the seemingly bottomless doggie dish of water, Marta's voice returned in her earphones. "Remember, May, you are our sweet slut puppy. Two important things to remember: One, you are ours to use as we please. We'll think seriously about enjoying your slutty holes for our pleasure later. I know you're dripping wet right now. Two, you are a mere pup. If you need something, you'll let us know the way any other dog would. The gag stays off, and you are free to express yourself, but not with words – with sounds like a dirty little mutt would make. Bark loudly if you understand."

May turned red as she cried out, puppy style.

The voice of her owner continued on: "Remember, slut puppies can't come without permission, so you'll have to be creative in your begging, little pup."

Seconds later, May felt a hand around the belt on her waist pulling her ass closer to one end of the cage. Using the belt, Ophelia was positioning May's ass in such a way that she would have access to the slut puppy's tight asshole. The puppy cocked her head to one side, trying to see or hear what was happening behind her, but before she had a moment to speculate, she felt cold lube running down her ass crack and creeping towards her pussy. Something cold and hard was being pressed against her rosebud. It was glass maybe. Or metal. She wasn't sure, but she yelped and whimpered suddenly at its eventual invasion and final resting place.

Plugged and horny, the slut puppy was rocking on all fours now. While rocking she felt something soft brush back and forth against her thigh, and realized that the plug in her ass was actually a tail. She wanted something in her pussy. Almost bad enough to break good form and protocol and Tetris herself onto her own fist right then and there. But that would be foolish. There would be no real reward in such disobedience. So instead, she rocked and whined and enjoyed the experience of the new appendage extruding from her ass.

This was not Tuesday.

Time passed on as music played, lending no hint as to how long May actually remained caged and ignored. It was in her solitude that she was unable to deny the growing need to pee. When holding it became less of an option, May knew what she had to do. She needed to get the attention of her owners.

"ARF! ARF!" May called out loudly, followed by yelps and whines designed to grab the attention of her nearby owners.

Someone leaned in close and rubbed her neck gently, and then through the music May heard Ophelia's voice asking, "What is it, pup? What do you need, girl?". May danced and wiggled in the cage, whining pathetically until one of her owners guessed correctly that making pee-pee was what the puppy needed most of all. Marta slid a puppy pad under the still-blindfolded May, and the embarrassed puppy whimpered herself into many shades of red as she relieved herself there in a cage, piss running down her legs.

Through the cage behind her, she felt and recognized the appearance of something less foreign to her. A Magic Wand was being fed through the bars. She felt it touch her thigh a time or two. Unsure of whose hands were fastening it to her left thigh with straps, she wriggled and moaned like a bitch in heat. A fast slap on her ass calmed her and the message was received. She remained still.

A voice again! This time, it was Ophelia in her ear practically whispering, "Enjoy it, sweet slut. Come freely until we say no more. You've earned it. This is your fiftieth Tuesday with us, and so to celebrate, we've thrown you a dinner party. By the way, our guests are enjoying you. Don't disappoint."

May's breathing increased rapidly at the discovery she was in company she had never met before. On display. A show dog. A slut puppy caged and ignored while she was unaware of being at the centre of dinner and merriment. SO many emotions. Terror and excitement danced with one another as the slut became turned on to the point of growling. Marta paused the playlist so May could hear the reactions of the guests for the first time.

She returned to rocking, followed by whimpering and finally howling. She was begging. Begging for an orgasm. Begging for the humiliation. Wanting it. Desperately. A voice she didn't recognize suggested she didn't want it bad enough. She growled, and snarled, then yelped and howled sorrowfully.

Click.

The Magic Wand was flipped on the high setting and May was jolted to the point of jumping, nearly breaking the flimsy dog kennel. Her front paws collapsed under her, which pushed her ass up even higher.

Howling uncontrollably while trying to ignore the flood of tears now soaking her blindfold, May growled and panted and yelped her way through orgasm after orgasm. Quivering beneath the almost unbearable vibrations on her clit, May was pleasantly surprised at the sudden presence of a gloved hand fondling and teasing her cunt. With the Wand still buzzing like a champion, the hand easily penetrated the wanton slut's juiciest hole.

She was an insatiable slut puppy. Her sex juices now mixing with the piss that soaked the pad underneath her, she wanted to stop, but it was hard to imagine it ever ending. May tried to guess how many people were watching her being fucked like an animal in a cage, and that only made her hungrier for more. Eventually, her knees gave out beneath the quivering intensity of the last big gush, and a sloppy wet hand popped from her pussy.

Marta bent down near her head and spoke. "You're such a good little slut puppy. A greedy little bitch. You did well. I think it's safe to say we are all pleased with you." May felt her blindfold being removed. Her head was on the bottom of the cage, her ass still dangling ungracefully in the air, and for the first time, she saw her audience.

Giggles erupted as she blushed from head to toe.

As the six guests all said their goodnights and offered their appreciation, they reached through the cage to scratch the puppy behind her ear on the way out. May was exhausted and so pleased.

Ophelia recognized the sleepy look in her eyes. "Not yet, sleepy little slut puppy. We aren't quite finished with you. I'm going to let you out, and you'll go to our bedroom and fetch your favourite cane. Bring it back and be quick about it!"

When the cage door was unlocked, May found the strength to bolt forth excitedly. She hated nothing more than being a disappointment. Pleasing was her specialty. She returned with a blue acrylic cane between her teeth and presented it to Ophelia.

What followed were fifty strikes of the cane on the puppy's tender flesh. "One for each week you've been with us," said Marta. "Just think, next Tuesday you get to take fifty-one."

"Next Tuesday," thought May. "I wonder what next Tuesday will bring." And with that thought, she was placed back into the cage, her face now at the opposite end, and her nose shoved into the wet mess that she made. This is where she slept that night.

The next morning, May didn't make breakfast. At her owners' insistence, they did the cooking. May stayed chained to a chair leg, and happily ate the bacon from her dog dish beneath the table.

No, that was not at all a Tuesday like the ones May had grown to love. Perhaps she could be excited about the unfamiliar, after all.

Affinity & The Spit

Artist: Toby Wiggins

Toby Wiggins (or simply "Wiggins") is a PhD student and artist living in Toronto, Ontario. Working and studying at York University in Gender, Feminist and Women's Studies, Wiggins's areas of interest include sexualities, perversion, trans studies, queer theory, psychoanalysis, and affect. In particular, their work looks at BDSM and feminist cultural production as a site of theory and resistance. Wiggins is also a documentary filmmaker, pornographer, and multimedia artist. They directed and produced the feature documentary *Nourish Peterborough*, which followed several grassroots anti-poverty organizations advocating for food security and sovereignty in their communities. Currently, along with DIY art porn production, Wiggins is teaching undergrads about gender, and running a seminar in psychoanalysis and perversion through FAG's (Feminist Art Gallery) freeschool. They also love taking walks with their adorable miniature poodle, Gratch.

Wiggins's photos in the kinky Toronto anthology mirror the intimacy of the queer BDSM community, the beauty of marginalized sexuality, and the magic of chosen family.

I have never met Wiggins's poodle Gratch, which is a shame, but I have had the pleasure of sitting on the same panel as Wiggins at the most recent Unholy Harvest, and hear them talk about the connections between kink and their academic life, which was a delight. I was enchanted to receive the hot picture Wiggins contributed.

Affinity

The Spit

Under Her Boot

Squeaktoy

Squeaktoy is a relative newcomer to the Toronto women's Leather scene but from the moment the door was opened to her she has felt welcomed and a part of this diverse family. This story is her favourite fantasy subject: the idea of being at the boot of a beautiful woman does all kinds of bad things to her, such that if all goes well she will be able to experience it again soon. Squeaktoy runs a monthly discussion group on power exchange, tPEG, and has presented at the Playground Conference in Toronto. This year will be her first IMsL and she is looking forward to expanding her role in the Ontario Leather scene in the days/months/years to come.

Before I met Squeaktoy, I was wondering what the squeak was all about in her chosen name. Then I heard her...

I chose her story "Under Her Boots" because of the way it describes the kind of encounter that could happen at any play party, and yet one that is special and shows how something can really occur between two individuals who have just met, and who consent to a particular kind of intimacy for the duration of a scene.

I see her across the room and my stomach clenches.

That's unusual.

She's with people I don't know well but I make my way over. Why not? It's time. I'm hungry. And my new leather is making me bold. I join the conversation, quietly. Playing the good girl. Watching her face to see how she responds. She blushes. I gesture at the whip on her belt.

"You any good with that?"

"Not bad. Wanna go?"

I glance back at her face – I like what I see. Eyes alive at the prospect of hitting a pretty girl. "Sure, why not?" And we break away from the group. Negotiations begin.

I don't tell her I'm a masochist but I can see that she's a sadist and I'm pretty sure she can read me too – it's like we thrum at a different vibration from the rest of the world. Or maybe it's the way our eyes light up at the prospect of pain, giving and receiving.

Face slapping, no-go zones, punching, kicking, I don't do well with slappy but thuddy is good. Sex is cool. "I might even like it." I like my boundaries pushed but I'll use my safewords if I need them. Yellow means please check in, red stop that. "I swear, hope that's okay?"

Crash – she's fucking slapped me! Then she grabs me by the hair and twists me onto my tiptoes, growling into my ear, "No, swearing is not okay, bitch. Remember that." And she throws me to the ground.

Fight or flight kicks in. New leather, dirty floor? "Fuck you!"

Instantly her boot is into my ribs, moving me several feet along the dirty floor. Can't. Breathe.

Pain shatters through the haze as she grabs my hair, not by the roots, so it's going to come right off my head! "You fucking bitch! What the fuck!"

Red shattering welt breaking darkness as my body hits the wall. Crumple to the floor only to feel her boots on my right thigh, left arm, ass, stomach, nowhere is safe as I try to find an escape.

Then a boot on my face, so hard that I can feel every tread. Fuck, are those spikes? She'll scar me! Still, so still. I can't move. Fear is the only thing in the world. She presses harder.

"No. Swearing."

"I promise, I promise, please, please stop!" I hear myself begging thinking in the back of my mind we didn't negotiate *this*.

"Please what?"

"Please, Sir, please. I won't swear, I promise, Sir!" The boot is lifted the smallest bit. Thank god. "Thank you, Sir. I'm sorry, Sir!"

She lifts me to my feet then twists my arm behind me, too tight! It'll break! No!

Mouth beside my ear she whispers, "Swear again and you won't like my reaction nearly that much."

And I almost can't not swear.

But I don't and she releases my arm. "Get naked," she instructs me. And turns and walks away.

I can feel energy moving through my veins. I am alive. I am drenched. I move to the chair, obediently removing my skirt (how did it get wrapped around my waist?), stockings, top. I don't know what happened to my shoes. Don't care. I look around for her as my hands fumble behind my back with my bra strap.

"Who said you could take your fucking time?" My hands trapped, cuffed, face pressed into the wall before I can get my bra off.

"Too bad, it was pretty," she says and all I can see is a massive hunting knife held up to my face. I close my eyes as it traces my face, neck stretching to escape its touch, shoulder pulling away all the way to the middle of my back.

"Anything you want to say?" she asks.

"No, Sir," I choke out. "Please."

"Please what?"

"I'm sorry I was so slow, Sir."

She lets go of my wrists, places each hand on the wall, now I am holding myself there. The knife begins its journey again, I can feel it tracing a line through a thin layer of sweat. The back bra strap pulls as she slices through it. Then the shoulder straps. She pulls it off slowly, I hear it fall. Feel the knife travelling down my spine. I hold myself tightly to the wall. *Breathe*, I remind myself as I feel her breath on the small of my back. *Breathe*. Every sensation twice as strong as usual.

She cuts off my panties, pulls them off and chuckles. "You fucking masochist," she laughs shoving them in my mouth. This was definitely not negotiated, I tell her with my eyes, shaking my head, no, no. "Spit them out if you need to talk," she says. "But it had better be important."

Fear again. Knees weaken.

She grabs my hair, pulls me away from the wall and thrusts me toward a spanking bench. Lays me across it instead of having me kneel. "Stay," she says.

Like I could move.

My stomach rests on the cool vinyl. My ass out in the air feels especially naked. She comes around and crouches in front of me. Takes my right hand and places a length of chain attached to the bench in it. Then repeats this with my left hand. She stares at me – likes what she sees?

"When you need it to end let go of the chains," she says. Waits until I nod then walks around to the other side. I can hear a bag unzip, sense her laying toys on the bench. "Don't knock them off," she says. I nod. Mouth so dry I couldn't talk even without panties in my mouth.

What have I gotten myself into? Such. An. Idiot. I *asked* for this. I shake my head. My knees are shaking. I couldn't stand now if I wanted to.

Behind me she grabs my hips and pulls them back from the illusion of safety provided by the bench. "Spread them," she tells me as she kicks my feet apart. "Nice," she tells me. I am blushing, can barely hear her. Naked and exposed for everyone to see.

She thrusts three fingers into me and I can't not move, I'd cry out if I could. I didn't know I was that wet. She's in up to her knuckles, she almost reaches my clit as she pushes into me harder. Then she leans across my back. "You love it, you fucking slut." My tears tell her she is right. "Do you want to come?" She asks, pushing hard into me. I'm sobbing and nodding. God *yes*! I want to come.

"Too bad!" And she's gone. No weight on my back, no fingers wiggling in me. It takes everything I have to stay still and I realize that I am gripping the chains so tightly that they are hurting me. I try to lighten my hold, feeling bereft.

Crack. A leather strap on my ass breaks through everything. Again. Again. More sound than pain but the world is reduced to my ass and the anticipation of the next strike. Whack across my shoulders and I am so surprised I almost drop the chains. Again! Fuck! I struggle, writhing, knowing that it won't help. But I can't stay still.

And then...

CRACK.

Can't breathe. Can't take it. The world reduced to a line of searing red pain across my upper thighs. The sweet spot.

Rewarded by her hand pressing on the welt. "Oh that's a nice one." And I breathe. Until she lifts her hand and slaps me right on the welt. Twice. I kick out, unable to hold back. And am punished with a flurry of blows to my legs. No pattern, no remorse she hits me again and again until I am sobbing, snotty, unable to breathe.

"Take out the gag." Did she say that? Someone pulls the panties out of my mouth, roughly wipes tears and snot mostly off my face.

Thwack.

Oh god is that a cane? Smaller, searing lines take over my consciousness. I stomp and dance but keep my feet close to the ground. No more kicking.

She leans down in front of me. Tilts my face up, looks into my eyes. "You're a quick study," she says. "No more kicking," she laughs.

Then. "You ready for more?" Unbelievably, I nod. She releases my face, goes to the side.

Two canes beat a pattern on my back. Gentle, repetitious. I am relaxing into it, concentrating on the shimmer in my veins. The pain retreats when I focus on the shimmer, the feeling of stars shooting through my body. A slight hesitation in the canes pulls me out slightly but then the rhythm continues. A little harder, a little faster. A little more uneven.

Thwack!

Fuck! My whole body lifts from the bench, landing again I slide in the wetness that has come from my body. I can't see. How can she be two places at once? The canes change again, one then the other, seemingly determined to reach the bench beneath my body. And...

Thwack!

Across my thighs this time. And I scream out, losing count of the canes on my back broken by something leather on my ass and thighs. Two of them. There must be.

Thwack!

Two of them. The bastard.

Thwack!

Screaming, struggling shouting for her to stop, for mercy, begging and then no words just sounds.

Trying to get away but there is nowhere to go, the world reduced to a square of maybe six feet. Dimly I can sense there are others but they don't factor in. Only the hands that wield the canes and the leather.

Then blessedly the leather stops, the canes slow down to the most rhythmic drumming, I can do this. I can do this. Hands force my legs apart, thighs slick with sweat and excitement I am ashamed momentarily of being so excited except that's the right response as she shoves her cock all the way in and again and again.

When she is done, she laughs and slaps my ass before moving away. And I lie there on the bench utterly spent as I realize that I can let go of the chains now. I'm ready for it to end.

No Translation Necessary
Traduction superflue
JoNi

Jo and Ni are a butch-femme/top-bottom couple who are regular riders of the rails in the Montreal/Toronto corridor. For this story, they put their pens together for the first (but not the last!) time. You can read their previous writings scrawled on bathroom walls, on balled-up restaurant napkins, and in shoebox love letters if you care to do your detective work. They believe in the power of language (both spoken and unspoken), and in the power of power itself.

I was very happy to receive this bilingual short story that vividly translates the kind of erotic exchanges that occur between Toronto and other Canadian and Québécois cities – here, Montreal. Of course, it also clearly conveys both the francophone and francophile presence in Toronto.

Jo et Ni forment un couple *butch-femme/top-bottom* faisant régulièrement usage du train dans le corridor Montréal-Toronto. Elles rédigent ici à quatre mains pour la première fois, mais certainement pas la dernière! Vous pouvez tenter de retracer leurs œuvres griffonnées sur les murs des toilettes publiques, gribouillées sur des serviettes de table ou encore, cachées dans des boîtes à double fond. Elles croient en la puissance des langues (quelles qu'elles soient) et en la force du pouvoir.

J'ai été très heureuse de recevoir cette nouvelle bilingue qui transmet de manière éloquente le type d'échanges érotiques qui surviennent entre Toronto et les autres villes canadiennes et québécoises – ici, Montréal. Évidemment, cela transmet également très bien la présence francophone aussi bien que francophile à Toronto.

Samedi matin, 10 h. Je suis arrivée à Toronto la veille, par le train de 22 h. Épuisée, je me suis rendue directement à mon gîte où je me suis endormie peu de temps après. C'est la faim qui m'a réveillée et éjectée du lit; une chance que le B&B où je loge inclut le déjeuner. Mais quant au café, il me faudra trouver autre chose... Infect! Première différence majeure entre Montréal et Toronto... Je quitte le gîte pour visiter la ville, tout en obsédant sur un vrai café. Après m'être promenée tout l'après-midi, je trouve un restaurant où je me pose pour déguster un bon souper. Mais l'envie d'un café digne de ce nom m'obsède maintenant. Je reprends ma visite jusqu'à ce que je voie une enseigne inspirante : Café Baristacrat. Est-ce le mot « café », ou le fait qu'il soit épelé en français qui m'a attirée, je ne saurais dire. Je pousse la porte et l'odeur de café me séduit immédiatement. Je m'avance vers le comptoir et la serveuse accroche mon regard : une magnifique Femme impeccablement vêtue sous son tablier, portant longue la chevelure bouclée et affichant un sourire irrésistible. Je tente de cacher mon émoi, mais je sens néanmoins une rougeur envahir mon visage. Je déteste quand cela arrive... va-t-elle s'en rendre compte? Malgré le comptoir, grâce à ses talons hauts, je peux apercevoir son décolleté… et mon regard a dû errer un peu trop longtemps car, en prenant ma commande, elle se penche de façon séductrice et mentionne quelque chose en anglais que je ne saisis pas. Mais son ton me laisse deviner qu'elle me taquine. Je prends le café auquel j'ai rêvé toute la journée et je vais m'asseoir un peu plus loin, de façon à continuer à l'observer plus attentivement. Wow! Quelle beauté! Et tellement sexy! Tout à fait mon genre! Comme accueil, je ne pouvais espérer mieux, même si nous n'avons guère échangé que quelques mots (que je ne suis pas sûre d'avoir compris — je dois vraiment me mettre à l'anglais). Je me demande si elle habite près d'ici et si je la croiserai à nouveau, à la fin de son quart de travail… Mon esprit vagabonde un long moment, puis je sors fumer un cigarillo, en continuant de rêvasser à ce qui pourrait se passer entre nous. C'est alors que je vois la belle sortir. Je devine qu'elle a terminé sa journée et j'ai envie de la suivre, pour voir où elle va… juste pour voir…

†††

Another day slinging late afternoon lattes at the Baristacrat. Four years of university, and it's come to this. But what else am I going to do with a bachelor's degree in psychology? It was either this or wait tables at the local beer hole, and I don't have the patience for that many assholes. At least I have the bitter aroma of my favourite Colombian blend to keep me company on this shift – and some of the customers can be amusing, on a good day.

Today might be one of those days, I'm thinking, as I watch the cutest boi, fiercely intent on the menu on the wall above me, shuffle slowly forward in line. There's something about her that's… well, hot! She has a shaved head, motorcycle boots and a tight body, and as she gets closer I notice her melt-worthy chocolate brown eyes. Ahem! Anyway… When she reaches the counter, I lean over it and say, "What can I do for you today?" The boi looks up at me (I notice I'm a good foot taller than her in my heels), and begins to bluster, red-faced. "Euh… A coffee?… coffee strong, please?" I hear the adorable French accent, and detect the faint scent of something slightly sweet… and smile just a little. Just a little, mind you. It takes a lot to melt this fierce femme's heart.

I look down at her, letting her flounder just a little bit longer. I realize she wants a coffee. Grade school French classes got me that far, but I like watching that blush creep along her jawline. Finally, I decide to save her. "How about a Colombian dark roast? We've got my favourite brewing today." Seeming to understand, she nods in relief and puts her money on the counter as I pour her a cup of the rich blend. When I hand over the steaming cup, our fingers brush lightly. An electric charge pulses between us in the brief moment the coffee changes hands. Nearly

153

blushing myself now, I quickly cover and turn to serve the next customer.

When I turn back, she's seated by the door, slowly sipping... and staring at me unabashedly. What a bold, impertinent boi! Again I busy myself in order to hide the fact that this random, handsome stranger is putting me a bit off balance. It's a busy Saturday so it's easy to keep myself occupied, though every once in a while I sneak surreptitious glances the boi's way, just to see if she's still hanging around. She remains at the same spot as an hour, then two go by, even though her cup looks like it's long empty.

As the clock edges towards 11 pm, the nighttime coffee crowd thins out. I breathe a sigh of relief when my shift ends. Shrugging off my apron, I grab my coat and look expectantly towards the table the boi has been stationed at all night – and to my disappointment, she's nowhere in sight. I mentally berate myself for not making my interest more apparent – and now it's too late. "Damn, girl!" I mutter under my breath, pushing open the shop door a little more vigorously than necessary.

Turning for home, I barely register a sweetness on the air... almost like the boi had left a piece of herself there, just to tease me. She's probably an asshole, anyway. I mean, what kind of person stares down someone for two hours, only to leave without a word?! My boot heels crunch in the fall leaves as I make my way to the "shortcut" (really a long cut) that I take through the Don Valley to get to my apartment. As crazy as life can get sometimes, this walk through the woods never fails to put me in a calmer place — and at this time of night, there's never anyone around, the bikers and joggers being long gone. Flicking on my flashlight and sighing, I decide to chalk up tonight as a missed opportunity that will present itself again if it was meant to be. The deeper I get into the woods the less disappointed I am, and the more this makes sense. I mean, things happen exactly the way they're supposed to, right?

Suddenly, I hear a branch snap behind me. I realize quickly that I'd let my guard down while walking — very unusual for me. "Who's there?" I say, louder than necessary, given the quietness of the woods. I wait... but there's no answer. Maybe it was a squirrel or another animal, I'm thinking... Silly to be so paranoid. But still... my nerves are a bit on edge. I continue on my way, heading towards what I call the end of the rainbow. It's a tunnel with a rainbow painted around the outside edges. My ex-girlfriend used to call it that, somewhat sardonically, when we'd go walking together, and it stuck. After I've been in the tunnel for about a minute, I detect a faint echo of my clicking footsteps, vaguely off rhythm. Something is up, and I don't like this at all...

†††

J'ai à peine le temps de terminer mon cigarillo que je la vois sortir en coup de vent, manifestement agacée par quelque chose. Je lui emboîte le pas à travers un boisé très agréable, gardant une certaine distance pour qu'elle ne se sente pas suivie, mais pas trop loin pour bénéficier de la lueur de sa lampe de poche. J'essaie de ne pas faire de bruit, mais le sentier est jonché de feuilles mortes et de branches, que je ne peux empêcher de faire craquer sous mes bottes. Je me fais aussi discrète que possible, mais je vois bien qu'elle se retourne de temps en temps. Je ne veux pas l'effrayer... juste voir où elle va et... et quoi, au juste? Je ne saurais l'expliquer, mais mon petit doigt me dit que le risque en vaut la peine. C'est alors qu'elle entre dans un tunnel faiblement éclairé. Je continue de la suivre, entre dans le tunnel à mon tour, mais je ne la vois plus. Merde! Où est-elle passée? Elle ne peut pas s'être volatilisée.

†††

Nerves tingling and mind racing, I exit the tunnel and quickly flatten myself along the outside of the tunnel, shutting off my flashlight. I fumble for the hairstick I'd hastily put in this morning... It's a far cry from a weapon, but it's all I've got. As the fucker gets closer, I poise for action. I have no clue what I'm going to do — but when I see a darkened form leave the exit of the tunnel I leap forward, grab the asshole from behind, and press the tip of my "knife" into their neck. There's a choked sound, and just as I'm about to snarl something at them I realize — what the? — it's the same boi from the coffee shop!

I flip her around and turn the flashlight on directly in the boi's face. "You?! What the hell are you doing following me? Are you fucking *stalking* me?!" The boi stutters and fumbles her words, saying something in French that I don't understand. "What? Explain yourself to me, boi!"

Then her demeanor seems to change. She looks up at my face for a moment, and then lowers her eyes. Her cheeks redden, and she stammers, "… not scare you… did not mean this… want to meeting you." What the fuck is this about, I wonder. And just then, something clicks. This boi, this energy. I know this. I've just met her, and yet there's something familiar hanging between us. And with those flushed cheeks, those down-turned eyes, I think she knows me too.

†††

A la sortie du tunnel, je sens tout juste un mouvement derrière moi et une poigne solide m'agrippe par derrière, enfonçant quelque chose de pointu à la base de mon cou. Elle m'a fait la prise du lutteur et je ne peux plus bouger sous peine d'étouffer ou de me faire ouvrir la gorge. M'éclairant avec une lampe de poche, elle crie quelque chose que je ne comprends pas. Son ton oscille entre la peur et la menace avec un petit quelque chose que je ne saurais décrire… Serait-ce de l'excitation? Elle est définitivement en position de contrôle, et je ne peux que m'abandonner à son étreinte. Je bafouille quelque chose en anglais qui semble la calmer un peu, et elle abaisse son « arme » lorsqu'elle me reconnaît de notre brève rencontre au café.

Je reprends mon souffle et la regarde avec défi. Que pense-t-elle pouvoir me faire, vraiment? Mais une certaine crainte m'envahit néanmoins au regard qu'elle me retourne. Elle continue de me parler en anglais, de me dire ce qui semble être des insultes, ou des encouragements, je ne suis pas sûre. Je trouve tout cela absolument sexy… et terriblement excitant! Je baisse la tête, brièvement, juste assez pour qu'elle soit à nouveau sur moi et me fasse pivoter, tout en saisissant mes deux bras fermement avec son bras gauche. Elle m'attire dans le tunnel et me pousse face contre le mur, tout en tirant sur mon gilet. Elle me donne un ordre, qui trouve écho dans le tunnel, puis, voyant que je ne comprends pas, elle mime de baisser mon pantalon. Je lève les sourcils avec un air interrogateur, mais elle ne rigole pas. Je m'exécute, débouclant ma ceinture et laissant tomber mon jean jusqu'à mes chevilles, exhibant un boxer rouge illustré de condoms qui dansent. Une chance que j'ai mis de beaux caleçons! Elle ne peut réprimer un sourire, passe un commentaire avec le mot « cute », se reprend et m'ordonne d'enlever mon *jacket* (ça au moins, je le comprends). Je m'exécute et ne puis m'empêcher de faire une mini révérence en le déposant à ses pieds.

†††

My mind is whirling with the sudden possibilities of the situation – and with the realization that the boi

158

hadn't any intention of leaving the coffee shop without a word. But what a way to try to meet a woman — by scaring her half to death! From between clenched teeth, my words seethe anger I no longer truly feel. "So you think you can follow me here, scare the *shit* out of me, and get away with it? You think that's *acceptable* behaviour, boi?" Her cheeks become an even darker shade of red under the flashlight's glare, as she starts to speak and then simply shakes her head no. "You need some lessons in how to pick up a femme, boi! D'you hear me?" The boi looks up uncomprehendingly, and in answer I grab the front of her shirt and shove her backwards into the entrance of the tunnel. Back against the curved, concrete wall, she dares to look up at me with a hint of defiance in her eyes. "Oh no you *don't*, boi... Don't you dare!" Whether she understands my words or not, recognition flashes in her eyes... and do I detect a slight relaxing of her shoulders?

"Look at me," I order. When the boi looks up, I bark, "Pants down!" Her eyes widen, but she doesn't make a move. "Pull your *fucking* pants down, *now!*" My voice echoes in the tunnel in a way that amplifies the sound back to us. With my words still hanging in the air, the boi quickly fumbles with her belt, and pushes her jeans down to her ankles, awkwardly. I keep the flashlight trained on her movements, enjoying the spotlight effect it has. As she straightens up, I notice her boxers — red, with dancing condoms. "Real cute," I say somewhat sarcastically. The boi smiles shyly, as if I've just given her a compliment. Hmm... There's an enticing bulge, I notice, beneath the boi's boxers. I find myself tempted to take a peek, but stop myself. Must not get distracted. "Jacket off too!" I insist, watching her intensely. She shrugs the jacket off and lays it down with something close to reverence.

I look the boi up and down... legs awkwardly shackled by her own pants, the ridiculous underwear, plain white t-shirt. This boi is some kind of hot! Her nipples are hardening against the chilly air in the tunnel. I trace my fingernails across the side of her neck, causing her to shiver. This pleases me, and I continue to trail my nails down further, over the cotton of her t-shirt, until they reach her nipples. I will her to look up at me, and she does. I look into her eyes as I caress her nipples, feeling them harden further beneath my fingers. Still looking at her, I take both nipples between my fingers and twist. Hard. To the boi's credit, she doesn't cry out, but sucks in her breath and widens her eyes. I push my body into hers, knowing that the added advantage of my heels on top of my height places my cleavage directly below the boi's face. I feel her hips buck, and allow myself to smile, hidden from her view. Horny little fucker!

My hands move to her sides and slowly lift her t-shirt off. I scratch my nails along the tender flesh on her sides as I pull it up. She's topless, with her pert, small breasts exposed. I begin to play with my new toys. Tongue flicking, teeth nipping, pinching, scratching, I play with her chest as I feel the bucking of her hips grow a little stronger, and light moans begin to escape her lips. "You like it when it hurts, hm? You fucking pervert!" I reach my hand down, trailing past her hips and down to her inner thighs. She shivers again, in anticipation, as I finger the lovely, soft flesh there. I then grab some of that flesh and twist it cruelly. No sooner has the boi gasped than I start to pinch, scratch, and slap her thighs, drawing more gasps and moans.

I move in between her thighs and breasts, my cunt throbbing as I watch her skin become a mass of angry, red welts, and scratch marks. The boi's breath grows more and more ragged, but she hasn't once asked me to stop. I stop what I'm doing and look her directly in the eye. "Do you understand 'red'?"

She nods in understanding, "Rouge, oui."

"Ok, 'rouge' is the word… Rouge, okay?"

"D'accord, Madame," the boi replies, eyes lowered to me. I believe we have understanding.

I pull a bottle of water from my purse and offer her a drink. She gulps gratefully, and hands it back. "Merci," she almost whispers.

I take a swig myself and then order, "Turn and face the wall, boi!" The boi does just that, her chest still heaving slightly from my previous attention. Mmmm… She makes a great picture, standing against the wall. I survey the landscape of her back, searching for the perfect spot to start. I begin to massage the areas around her shoulder blades and neck. I feel her begin to loosen underneath my fingers, and hear her breathing return to normal again. I start lightly thumping her back with the palm of my hand, warming up the area, watching the skin slightly pink underneath my palms. She begins to breathe in long, slow breaths as I increase the force of my blows. Feeling somewhat meditative doing this, I take my time keeping to the rhythm I create, and listening to the boi's even breath. When I add in occasional punches and slaps her breathing changes, and again, those gorgeous hips start pumping. "Fucking masochist!" I whisper in her ear. She smiles. Maybe this is a phrase she's heard before…

✝✝✝

C'est alors qu'elle m'observe attentivement, de la tête aux pieds… un regard, oserais-je dire, appréciateur? Ses yeux s'arrêtent brièvement à mon boxer et je me demande si elle a deviné ce que je porte dessous. Peu importe, son inspection terminée, ses doigts, qui couraient le long de ma poitrine, empoignent fermement mes seins, les pinçant avec force. Je retiens mon souffle et mords l'intérieur de ma joue pour ne pas crier, ah ça, pas question! Ses doigts courent alors le long de mon cou, de mes côtes, et commencent à me pincer, me triturer, me griffer, jusqu'à ce qu'ils atteignent mes cuisses et me frappent,

162

doucement d'abord, puis de plus en plus fort, alternant entre mes fesses et mes cuisses. Je ne peux pas bouger, le béton écorchant mon dos, les pantalons immobilisant mes jambes. Mais est-ce que je me sauverais, vraiment? Je commence à vraiment apprécier mon séjour à Toronto… D'autant que quelqu'un peut survenir à tout moment et nous surprendre. Et si c'était un policier! Cela ajoute à l'excitation.

Elle plante alors ses beaux yeux verts (ou bleus?) dans les miens et me demande en anglais si je comprends le mot « red »… Si c'est bien ce que je pense, j'ai vraiment trouvé le *jackpot*! La première personne que je croise serait donc *kinky*? Wow! J'ai peine à y croire, mais c'est bien ce qu'elle me répète : « Ok, 'rouge' is the word… Rouge, ok? » « D'accord, Madame », je dis. Mais elle n'est pas à la veille de l'entendre, car, franchement, j'adore le traitement qu'elle m'inflige jusqu'à présent. Après m'avoir offert de l'eau, elle me fait à nouveau pivoter face contre le mur et masse mon dos, d'abord doucement, puis de plus en plus fermement, accélérant son toucher jusqu'à ce qu'il se transforme en coups. Ma respiration suit ses coups, inspiration, expiration, et mes hanches se mettent à bouger spontanément, naturellement. « Fucking masochist! », me chuchote-t-elle à l'oreille. Cette fois, je comprends très bien ce que cela veut dire et je souris. Ce n'est pas la première fois qu'on me traite de masochiste… et je le prends comme un compliment!

†††

I ramp up my pace, punching, slapping, and twisting her skin between my fingers until she gasps for breath. My hips join hers in their motion, and when I slam my body into the boi, she notices this. She murmurs something I don't understand, but I don't have the patience for translation right now. "It's time for this ridiculous underwear to come off," I say, starting to tug them down slowly, watching the boi's profile for any sign that this isn't okay.

"Oui, oui!" she gasps – and that's all the encouragement this femme needs to hear! Adding her underwear to the pile of clothing at her feet, I see the strap-on she's been wearing underneath. Interesting evening wear for a coffee date with yourself, I'm thinking...

I then take a good look at what turns out to be a fine, fine ass. "Perfect for a beating," I say out loud, and without any further warning, I land my first blow – a stinging slap that causes the boi to move her ass away from me, instinctively. "Don't you fucking move away from me, you hear? If you want me to stop, use your word – rouge. Understand?"

"Oui," the boi answers, and moves her ass obediently back in place.

Okay, then, I think to myself, and begin slapping, pinching, and punching her ass into sweet submission. As my blows gain in intensity and speed, the boi begins to cry out, but I don't let up. Her ass is red, edging on purplish in some areas, but she makes no further move away from my hands.

As I move one hand down to give her inner thighs some more attention, I see a long, silver line of excitement reflected in the flashlight's glow. It's flowing from her cunt, dripping down to the pile of clothing by her feet. "Oh motherfucker…" I whisper under my breath. This wasn't exactly in my plans for tonight — but then, what part of this *was*? In moments like these, it pays to be an over-prepared femme with a huge purse. I lean down and rummage through the contents of my bag until I locate the ziploc of supplies I keep in case of emergency. I grab a glove, condom, lube… and as I move to stand up, I spontaneously pull the belt out of the boi's jeans.

"Turn to face me," I order, pulling her shoulder back so she understands. The boi shuffles awkwardly around, pants still around her ankles. I finally get a look at what she's been hiding underneath those boxers; a firm cock, standing at attention, just begging to be touched. I kick the boi's legs apart to their maximum shackled width and tear the wrapper of the condom off with my teeth. She looks at me with hungry eyes as I roll the safe down over her cock. I slowly put on the glove, feeling the boi watching me from beneath her lowered lids. Then I pull out the belt, which gets a slightly less subtle reaction from the boi — her eyes widen and she lets out a small gasp before trying to choke the sound back. I wrap it around the boi's neck once, then indicate that she should hold one end, while I hold the other. My hand, I mime, will stay still, holding the belt. It will be up to her to tighten or loosen the tension on her neck. I motion that we will test this once, and the look that passes over the boi's face as she pulls the belt taut tells me my instinct was right when I grabbed it out of her pants at the last minute.

✝✝✝

Madame va de plus en plus vite dans ses coups, et continue de pincer ma peau ici et là jusqu'à ce que je sois à bout de souffle. Elle se met à bouger au même rythme que moi et à balancer son corps contre le mien. Je murmure à bout de souffle : « Ah oui, encore, encore Madame, s'il-vous-plaît, c'est si bon! » À son tour de me regarder sans comprendre, et elle n'insiste pas. Je sens sa main bouger vers l'intérieur de ma cuisse et, sentant la moiteur entre mes jambes, je m'interroge sur l'étendue de mon excitation. C'est avec un peu de gêne que je l'entends chuchoter « Oh motherfucker »… je devine alors que, comme d'habitude, je suis en train de laisser une trace! Je n'y peux rien, c'est tellement excitant! Incontrôlable…

Je sens son regard inspecter mes fesses… j'espère que je passe le test! J'entends des paroles rassurantes, puis je sens une douleur cuisante sur ma fesse et je bouge, instinctivement. Elle m'engueule et m'intime l'ordre de ne pas bouger ou d'utiliser le mot "rouge", ou du moins, c'est ce que je crois comprendre. J'acquiesce et me rapproche. Elle redouble d'intensité dans ses coups et un cri m'échappe, bien malgré moi. Je ne m'attendais pas à autant d'énergie, de fureur, de la part de cette Femme. Elle ne me lâche pas pour autant. Je sens mes fesses et mon dos devenir de plus en plus sensibles, mais pas question de bouger... No way!

Comme je m'interroge sur la suite, et sur le fait que je n'ai pas de gants à portée de main, je devine un mouvement derrière moi. Madame fouille à nouveau dans son sac, à la recherche de... quoi, au juste? Lit-elle dans mes pensées? Et qu'est-ce donc que ce cliquetis... ah non, pas ma ceinture! Moi qui jouis juste à entendre ce son... décidément, je pense qu'elle lit dans mes pensées, et qu'elle connaît mes moindres fantasmes.

Elle me fait tourner face à elle, difficilement à cause du pantalon toujours enroulé autour de mes chevilles puis, elle écarte mes jambes davantage, au maximum de ce que le jean permet. Je la regarde pendant qu'elle enfile lentement un gant de latex, puis un deuxième. Elle exhibe alors ma ceinture, me l'enroule autour du cou et me fait tenir une extrémité, pendant qu'elle contrôle l'autre bout. Elle me fait signe que c'est moi qui ai le contrôle de la ceinture, et du niveau d'étouffement que je désire. Je comprends immédiatement et tout cela envoie une onde supplémentaire d'excitation à mon clitoris, qui est gonflé à son maximum.

Elle se penche et saisit mon boxer pour l'enlever. Je pense : enfin! Et je lui signifie : « oui, oui! ». Il va donc retrouver le reste des vêtements à mes pieds. Elle découvre la raison du renflement du caleçon. J'exhibe, non sans fierté, un harnais affublé d'un dildo, tout dressé et prêt à l'action. Après un bref regard de surprise, elle fouille dans son sac et en retire condom et lubrifiant. Après avoir enfilé le condom, elle empoigne ma queue et se met à tirer dessus, à la pincer, à la masser, à la masturber, tout en continuant à pincer mes fesses et mes cuisses. Si je m'attendais à cela! Je bouge les hanches au même rythme que le va-et-vient de sa main et je sens que je deviens de plus en plus excitée. Elle va réussir à me faire jouir juste comme ça, juste là… Quand même, je dois me retenir. Mais je vois bien à son regard que c'est ce qu'elle veut. J'accélère donc le mouvement, de plus en plus, sentant tout mon corps se tendre et aspirer à la jouissance, qui explose soudainement, à grands coups de cris et de halètements.

††††

Holding the belt in place, my other hand travels down to the boi's cock and I begin to fondle it, causing the boi to make small grunting noises. Teasing her in this way for a while, I watch her face from time to time. We catch each other's eye once, and hold our gaze. This moment feels too intense for me though, and I have to cut my eyes away and focus on her cock, which I now begin pumping in rhythm to our quickening breath. The boi starts to thrust into my hand, her breath coming in short spurts and gasps. Her legs begin to tremble with effort and excitement, and I can see the climax building in the muscles of her body before it begins. I watch as the boi's face reddens and her mouth opens as the orgasm takes her over. Her hips buck in desperate thrusts as her cries echo and amplify in the tunnel. Intense! I smile at the power of doing this; of reducing this boi to grunts and thrusts, and to so much jelly in my hand. And this hand is nowhere near done for the night, I think as I smile to myself.

I let the boi catch her breath as I slip off the strap and pull down her cock, revealing what's underneath. My hand follows my eyes as they travel towards her cunt. My eyes widen as I feel the extent of her wetness. My hand immediately becomes slippery as it plays with her folds, teasing. The boi starts to whimper and gyrate her hips, wanting more, but I take my time as my fingers continue to learn the contours of this part of her body. I am also enjoying the small, animal-like sounds she's beginning to make. Oh, how I love to tease! My one finger begins to circle around the edges of the boi's cunt, drawing something close to a cry from her. I can feel her muscles clenching. I join a second finger in the circular motions and then, without warning, plunge these fingers into her cunt. So warm and dripping wet

– incredible! The boi is crying out as I immediately begin to slam into her, hard and fast. I feel the tension on the belt tighten in my hand as she pulls on her end, causing her breath to rasp in her throat.

†††

Comme si elle avait compris, sa main glisse vers mon sexe et ses yeux s'agrandissent en sentant la moiteur de celui-ci. A quoi s'attendait-elle au juste? Son doigt entreprend de me toucher légèrement, en effectuant des cercles qui agacent plus qu'ils ne satisfont, mais je sens que c'est bien ce qu'elle désire m'infliger comme supplice supplémentaire. Je gémis doucement pour l'encourager à continuer, en espérant que c'est ce qu'elle fera. Sans avertissement, elle plante deux doigts à l'intérieur et je ne peux retenir un cri de surprise et de jouissance à la fois. Elle plonge de plus belle en moi, de plus en plus fort, de plus en plus vite. Je tire sur la ceinture, décuplant le plaisir en coupant l'oxygène, émettant des râlements qui semblent lui plaire autant qu'à moi.

†††

Inspired, I add a third finger in her cunt, and resume my hard, rhythmic fucking. With my thumb, I flick her clit and feel it harden. The boi's breath returns in desperate gasps as she loosens her grip on the belt. We fuck and choke, fuck and choke, building in intensity to the point where we're both gasping for air, with rivulets of sweat running down our bodies. As I continue to fuck her, I recognize a change in her cunt. "No you don't!" I order.

This causes the boi's head to snap up, "Non?"

"No, not until I say yes... um, oui, understand?"

"Oui," says the boi obediently, if not happily so. I slow down my fucking momentarily, to allow us both to catch our breath. And as I begin to ramp up again, I lean forward and find her breasts with my mouth. She moans as I tease and flick her nipples with my tongue, pinch her skin between my teeth, and continue to fuck her with renewed intensity. I feel her body build up again. "Madame?" the boi cries, "Madame, s'il- vous-plaît?"

I know she's begging me, and I *do* like the way she calls me Madame, but I'm not through with her yet. I keep the intensity up, and look her directly in the eyes, "Non!" The boi's eyes widen with a look somewhere between hate, fear, and desire. God, I love that look! I continue pumping into her, intermittently flicking her clit, torturing her tits, and watching her face, enjoying the look that has come over it as she concentrates desperately on obeying me. So fucking precious...

†††

Je sens alors plus de doigts me pénétrer et mon Dieu, qu'elle y va, profondément et intensément, jouant du pouce sur mon clito en même temps qu'elle me baise. Je respire de plus en plus vite, je serre et relâche la ceinture, et respire, et serre, et relâche. L'intensité augmente tout comme le ruissellement de notre sueur sur notre peau. Je la sens comme je sais qu'elle me sent... c'est tellement bon! Mais je sens aussi que je vais jouir si elle continue, et elle aussi. « Non, pas maintenant » - me dit-elle en anglais.

« Ben là! », que je dis... Pas facile! Elle ralentit alors la cadence, se penche vers mes seins qu'elle embrasse et triture, et reprend le va et vient en moi, comme si cela allait aider à calmer mon excitation. Je gémis et quémande presque : « Madame, s'il-vous-plaît? »

Elle ignore mes appels et ne cesse de me baiser en m'interdisant de jouir, tout en vissant son regard au mien pour s'assurer que j'ai bien compris. Je pourrais prétendre ne pas comprendre, mais non... j'aime mieux jouer ce jeu que celui de la barrière des langues. Et parfois, toute traduction est illusoire. Seul le sentiment importe, surtout lorsqu'il est exprimé aussi intensément. Malgré le fait que nous ne nous connaissons pas, je sens que s'installe une chimie, une réelle communication non verbale avec cette Femme magnifique, rencontrée par hasard. Et je veux goûter chaque instant! Chaque plaisir en son temps!

✝✝✝

Okay, I think, and I begin to slam into her as hard as I can. "Oui," I say.

"Oui?!", the boi gasps. "Oui?" she says again, as if she's afraid she heard me incorrectly.

I look her directly in the eyes, arm pumping, and say it again – "Oui." The boi's eyes roll back into her head in her relief, and I feel her body start to tense in anticipation. I gasp as I feel her cunt change around my fingers. I feel warm liquid pool around my hand as her body begins to tense... and here it comes... hot damn! The boi screams out as her cunt squeezes my fingers tight. Pulsing waves carry me on the journey with her as she gasps and cries, body bucking, breath rasping, hips gyrating desperately. The climax seems to go on forever... unbelievable. And as she appears to come down a little, I renew my hard and fast fucking, to be rewarded with more of the same – amazing! Just... amazing.

†††

Comme elle accélère son mouvement, je l'entends dire : « Oui! ». « Oui? Vraiment? » je rétorque. Et elle répète: « Oui! », tout en continuant son mouvement en moi. Ah, enfin! Je peux enfin me laisser aller, complètement. Tous mes muscles se bandent, tout comme mon clito, qui va exploser bientôt. Je sens une fontaine sortir de mon vagin tellement je suis excitée. Et... oui... ça y est, je viens, je viens! Ahhh! C'est fou! La tête me tourne tellement je jouis intensément.

†††

I can feel her body relax now, her cunt opening and loosening around my fingers, and I sense my moment. I drop the belt, reach down and grab the lube by my feet, and add a generous amount in my hand. The boi, lost in her body still, barely notices what I'm doing. I wait for a moment, catch the boi's eye, and plunge deep within her. She screams, more out of shock than pain – I could feel she was ready for this.

†††

Je sens tous mes muscles se relâcher, incluant mon con, qui semble s'ouvrir davantage pour accueillir encore plus de doigts, plus d'elle en moi. Encore une fois, elle semble sentir le tout, car, après un regard, elle enfonce toute sa main à l'intérieur. Je crie, mais plus sur le coup de la surprise que de la douleur. J'étais tellement prête pour elle!

†††

My hand curls inside her, and I begin to slowly rock my fist. When I feel her body accommodate me fully, I begin to gently pump my hand, and feel her cunt answering in return. This boi is incredible! I can feel her body tensing in readiness. Her climax is so powerful that I have to struggle to keep my fist inside her, her muscles pushing and pulsating all around me. Her cries echo in the tunnel, and in my ears. Un-fucking-believable! As the spasms slow, I gently pull my hand out, feeling a momentary loss as it becomes fully my own once again.

†††

Sa main en moi me coupe complètement le souffle. Mélange de jouissance intense et de douleur, impression de remplissage, de complétion, de tout, d'intimité suprême. Elle est en moi, je suis autour d'elle, unies, ensemble, nous bougeons au même rythme, jusqu'à ce que la jouissance m'envahisse à nouveau et que l'écho de mes cris emplisse le tunnel. J'éjecte doucement sa main et ressens un vide incroyable, en même temps que le souvenir d'elle est encore présent en moi. Ouf! Je reprends mon souffle, à grandes goulées, et je glisse le long du mur jusqu'au sol.

†††

On being released, the boi sinks to the floor, breathing heavily. I fish for my water bottle again, offering her a drink. She smiles and gulps gratefully, handing the bottle to me for the final drink. I join her on the ground. We smile at each other, and then laugh spontaneously, and just a bit awkwardly. What happened was so intense, what do you say to each other after that? *Especially* when you don't speak each other's language. Right now, though, it feels good to just sit here, coming slowly back to earth.

†††

Madame m'offre à boire, ce que j'accepte avec volupté, lui rendant la bouteille d'eau pour la dernière gorgée. Nous sommes toutes deux assises par terre, épuisées, et nous éclatons de rire, d'un rire un peu nerveux qui survient lorsque deux personnes ne se connaissant pas viennent de connaître un moment intime et intense. Qu'ajouter à cela? Surtout quand on ne parle pas la même langue? On reste là, tranquilles, à se sourire et à rire, et c'est bon.

†††

As the boi leans her head back against the tunnel wall and closes her eyes, I realize that the first light of day has entered the tunnel. Have we really been here all night?! As the boi lets out a deep breath, I look at her and smile. Seeming to feel my gaze, she opens her eyes and turns to me.

"Est-ce que tu fumes?" she asks. I don't understand, so she reaches inside her leather jacket and pulls out a pack of cigarettes.

"Ah, no… but you go ahead," I say, waving permission. She lights the cigarette with a silver lighter she also pulled out of her jacket pocket and I immediately place the sweet, lingering scent from the doorway of the cafe. Nutmeg, or cloves. Something like that. I smile, realizing that she'd been waiting for me to leave. Planning this all along. Sneaky boi!

†††

La lumière du jour pénètre doucement à l'intérieur du tunnel, comme nous relaxons. J'ai tellement envie d'un cigarillo que je lui en offre un. Elle ne fume pas mais me fait signe que ça ne la dérange pas. Comme je m'allume, elle me regarde avec ses yeux pénétrants, comme si cette odeur lui était familière… Je lui rappelle peut-être une ex qui fumait le même type de cigarillo. J'espère juste que le souvenir lui est agréable. Il semble bien que oui, car elle sourit doucement.

†††

The boi looks at me. Her face seems to say, "Now what?" Now what, indeed. "Well," I say, "there's a great place I know, and it opens early. You might be familiar with it – Cafe Baristacrat?" Upon hearing the name of the cafe, the boi smiles, understanding my suggestion.

As we gather ourselves together for the walk back I smile to myself… I think we *do* speak the same language, after all.

†††

Nous nous regardons à nouveau, affichant un sourire niais. C'est alors qu'elle propose d'aller prendre un café… au Café Baristacrat! Pourquoi pas, me dis-je? Finalement, la langue n'est pas un obstacle à une certaine communication…

A Bump

Karl

Kate a.k.a Karl's leather life got its start in Orlando, Florida in the early nineties when she met her now-wife Jeanne. At that time, Jeanne and Kate were two of very few leather women in Central Florida. Along with Jeanne, Kate has attended leather events and functions too numerous to list. Stretching from Florida to New York, from Nova Scotia to Toronto, Ottawa, Montreal and places in between, if leather dykes are kinking it up you may find Kate, Karl or Speed among them.

I met Kate (or maybe it was Karl) in person only once, at An Unholy Harvest, but I am looking forward to meeting this shy yet determined sexy butch again. Meanwhile, I chose to publish her story because I enjoyed the flirtatious tone of it, and also its original *je ne sais quoi*.

O kay, here is a fantasy, or a wish maybe...

I have a little extra bit down below. It's a bit of skin just above my clit. I don't tell too many people unless they are going to be very close and sexually involved. I never thought much of it, I just call it my bump. It's very, very sensitive! I don't like anybody to touch it. I always keep a little hair there to kind of cover and protect it. I did have a girlfriend once who really liked it. She had red thick lips, sometimes she would hold me down and kiss it. I would freeze because it goes from pleasurable to really painful in an instant. But it felt good when she would gently kiss and caress it.

So the fantasy is. . . I am changing clothes for some reason with my friend J and her friend Y. They are both very lovely and have lots of delicious, plump, soft fem curves. J and her friend Y speak French and I do not. As we are changing Y says something to J in French, some conversation takes place. I don't think much about it but keep undressing. Then it occurs to me they are talking about me. Then the fear comes they are talking about my bump! J knows about and she is aware I don't like it touched, but her friend is very interested. They continue to speak in French, then I notice a change in their demeanor, suddenly J is pushing me back and I fall onto a bench. J is holding me down and her friend Y is spreading my legs, she starts to reach for and she touches my bump! It hurts at first then she starts to kiss it and to caress it with her tongue. The extreme pain starts to change to pleasure, I take my feet from her shoulders that I have been trying to push her away with and wrap them around her neck. I go from wanting to slap and punch her to wanting to hump her face. J is pressing me down and forcing her big boobs onto my face and into my mouth. I start to convulse and I feel I will suffocate under J's beautiful breasts! Then suddenly I shoot my load and come in Y's mouth! Y gets up and says something in French to J and they laugh. I am left feeling violated and liberated both, and a little in love.

This is my story fantasy dream. I am not a writer and must go jerk off now so I hope it makes you happy. Maybe someday I will show you my bump.

Boots on the Ground

Kitty Kavanaugh

The first time I saw Kitty, she was not aware that I was in the audience, watching her on stage doing things that made me think that she must be a very, very kinky girl. Which she certainly is.

Kitty Kavanaugh is a BDSM slave and writer from the East Coast with roots in the Toronto area. Having achieved success with her published works in the realm of non-fiction, Kitty has put her hand to pen and paper to bring some of her fictitious fantasies to the welcoming light of day. Her non-fiction articles have been based on her sexuality and experiences as a bisexual female youth and her deep-seated slavery embraced by the Leather community. Kitty has participated in Leather Pride events across the US and Canada, and continues to celebrate Leather Pride every single day in her walk.

About "Boots on the Ground," she writes: "I would like to dedicate this submission to my dear friend and mentor Mark 'Spanky' Bialous, Mr. New Jersey Leather 2008, who lost his battle to cancer in 2011. The world is less fabulous without you, girl. xoxo."

My mind is empty, as black and blank as the Boots before me. A swift tug to the chain between my attached nipple clamps prompts me to begin. I reach out and touch the cool leather for the first time since moving to Toronto. Work, play, and spiritual fulfillment pushed me to this place, but left me with a sense of natural uneasiness that I would cure, *now that I've got my boots on the ground*.

Naked and kneeling with my hands placed behind my back, I lower my head to gently kiss the familiar leather. As I moisten the Boot with each kiss, the cordial tapping of a rubber crop against my buttocks and thighs sends me dripping and my mouth watering. Working my way around the entire Boot, I finally use my hands, wrapping them around Their leg to pull myself into the Boot.

Joy fills me and my eyes cloud. Moistening my tongue and starting at the tip, I gently work at the Boot. I lick and savour the taste; a mix of my sweat, spit and tears. I catch any drips with my hungering tongue. I concentrate on the spots that bring the most pleasurable reactions from Them.

They shift Their feet, prompting me to move to the other Boot. I continue to worship, no longer held back by the distractions and stress of the move, consumed by the taste of the wax, the smell of the polish, the heat of my back, the shine of the Leather, and Their moans urging me to continue vigorously.

I can hardly breathe; my body aches to come under Their touch. Selfishly, I kneel, hands behind my back, gently place my forehead against the firm Boot and wait for further instruction. A soft pet to my head and a slow, encouraging pull to the chain of my nipples bring me to my feet. Motivating me to the bedroom, Their crop swiftly connects with my thighs and sends me scurrying to prepare to receive Them.

Miscellaneous

Master Malik

I had the good fortune to meet Master Malik last year when he came to town during the Toronto Leather Pride weekend to give a workshop on cathartic flogging.

He says he is a self-proclaimed nomadic Sufi who finds that living in Leather closely parallels his religious path. He discovered Leather in 1999 and embarked on the perilous journey of Mastery and slavery with his slave Cathy a couple of years later. Since that time Malik has presented on many SM and M/s topics in local, regional, national and international events; including Toronto which is like another home to him. Malik is co-owner of Xpressions in Tulsa, a sex positive dungeon for safe and comfortable SM and other scenes. He hopes that if you are in Tulsa, Oklahoma, you will come and visit. Meanwhile, feel free to visit his page: www.xpressionsoftulsa.com.

For Malik, passion is a force of life and the story included in this anthology (which happened in the beautiful city of Toronto) is an example of this. This passion came unbidden and unplanned, and the memories will not fade for a long time. The selection of short prose poem-style story that he chose to submit for the anthology is very different from the other texts, and yet burns with the same Leather essence. I hope it will touch your soul as much as it touched mine.

Elements of Soul

An ember, not realizing its own potential, exists in the heap of ashes, the live ashes, the sustaining and nurturing ashes. A glimmer, very light, almost below the level of registering. A puff of air glows the ember that appears henceforth as twinkle and spark and crackle.

A breeze feeds life into the glowing and sparkling ember and born there is a flame. The flame dancing, bluish at the bottom, yellow and alive, consuming the oxygen in the air, giving warmth and mesmerizing.

Another flame, born of another ember, is fed by the same air, stroked by the same breeze, nurtured with the same caring wind. It too dances and flickers and moves. One looks at these flames and wonders at the beauties that lie there. In time, these flames come together and now something else happens, an almost mystical phenomenon.

Drops of dew, children of fog, mysteries, hidden things, oscillate on the autumn leaves, leaves that will soon be free from their constraints. They blaze with colour and the moisture they contain. The fog lifts but the drops remain a while and the leaves dance in anticipation in the light breeze, the same breeze that gives life to the embers and flame and fire and elements of souls.

Embers, dewdrops, leaves, the changing of the seasons, wind and power and energy, visible and invisible, hidden and open, all this and much more, much much more. The dance of flames starts and continues. So are born elements of the souls, which are moist and warm and hot and soothing and all consuming at the same time.

Not forgetting the sighs and songs of the wind rushing through the trees and high grasses and a music which is comprised of not only sound but also colours and sight and warmth.

These elements of soul make the beings tremble... a shiver devoid of fear and full of, the best kind of all. The flames dance, flicker, move from side to side, high and low and sideways. Flames merge and separate and merge again, with the sizzle of drops of dew.

These flames are fed by light breezes that become gusts. All these elements feed on each other and are born of each other in this marvelous display of brilliance and thought and desire.

Wet Dreams [excerpt]

Some say that we don't dream in colour. I say, dreams are nothing but colours.

I awoke several times, or so I thought, and walked in a corridor between the dream world and a world where we both existed in a surreal manner, not denying each other. Yet in those moments, the dream world continued to beckon and made sure that there was no lasting interruption in the flow of colours and senses...

These were my worlds and I was the traveler, so this gives me the right to narrate them as I feel.

Remembering the tastes, smells, touches, caresses, breathing, inhaling, holding, exhaling, trembling and arching... remembering in the most fierce ways, still in the land of those marvelous and intoxicating dreams, that was the best part of this travel. These are songs of summer and falls, these are melodies of bumble bees ravishing the nectars of willing flowers, these are the slight breezes from the lands of our desires and passions.

Ecstasy and intoxication are the result, however fleeting it may be.

Moments

Two bodies become one, intertwining, merging, slithering and sliding with a music that is eternal and ever present. Eyes closed, opened or half opened, seeing and not seeing, turn inward with clarity of vision, or blurred by the veils of lust and passion.

Touch... yes, the touch of infinity and affinity, moving here and there then back, fingers, palms, soles, lips, not lingering at one place but like a butterfly, seeking, searching and consuming the nectar of love and desires.

Sighs, the unbidden, generated deep within, resonate with earth and sky and wind and fire...moans and words of no language reach toward the divine... calling and clutching and grabbing and holding on and staying there for eternity and such is the music of tunes uncaptured.

Urges, coded on our souls since the beginning of time, go much beyond the physical and the mechanical. Urges, the epitome of all, come rushing but not spilling or wasting, and in those rushes we find the tranquility and serenity of life and its starting point. These urges start from all points of body and mind, and once in motion, it is a sin to stop them -- for sin is lack of motion and lack of motion is death, and death is end of this life and this life, in all of its paradigms, is still precious and worth living.

Lines of colour of indescribable quality and shimmer, move back and forth with the speed of lust, passion and desire, merging, coalescing, spreading outward and inward. Their movements are of ancient times and memories and instincts, and like waves on the shore they crash and re-form with the same energy but further along. The waves grow higher and higher and stronger and stronger and the sounds of their crashes reverberate as if they came from indigenous drums and are never forgotten.

Breathing faster and faster and then forgetting to exhale, holding in all that is there and has been there. Bodies convulse, the mind loses its focus, the spirit soars and souls become one for a moment, or for eternity, a small death occurs and then life slowly comes back. Such are the moments and fruits of passion, lust and desires.

Love making [excerpt]

Not forgetting the scents and fragrances of these times of passion: the musky smells, the aroma of sweat and heat. These are purer than any perfume and cannot be sold in bottles and vials. There are flowers of the gardens and the wilds, and their scent attracts honey bees and birds. Here in the art of love making there are scents of bodies and juices and dripping and secretions and semen and even blood…and they attract angels and demons at the same time. And olfactory memory is one of the most powerful of them all.

Holiday

Marsha Clark

Marsha Clark is a visual artist living and working in Fredericton, New Brunswick. Her work is mainly in collage and painting and focuses on themes of identity, beauty and "otherness," as well as how our environment can shape our experience. She enjoys writing in her spare time, be it art reviews, short stories or erotica. You can see her portfolio at www.marshaclarkart.com.

When she was 18 she moved to Toronto to attend Ryerson University in the technical theatre program. It was in this big foreign city that she found her voice, her passion and her fascination with beautiful, odd things.

Her story was included in the anthology for its writing quality, of course, but also for the subtlety of the sentiments and actions it describes.

He walked into my life tired and frayed. His plane had arrived at Pearson that night and he was weary from travel. At first, he needed to vent about his job; the stress of being responsible for so many vulnerable employees, sensitive deadlines, so much money on the line – he felt totally overwhelmed and used up. Despite him being officially on vacation, his Blackberry kept buzzing and distracting him. Leftover work stress, marital troubles, ties to his "normal" life that could not be cut in the daytime had the potential to be put aside this night. I sat him on my couch, looked him in the eyes and touched his chest. "It's okay now. I'm going to take care of you. I'm going to help you feel good, I'm going to help you let go," and with that, I led him to my bedroom.

"Remove your clothes and kneel on my bed. Anything I do in this room is because I want to do it, not because you get pleasure from it – though that is a wonderful side effect, isn't it? You will do exactly what I tell you, or you will be punished. Understand?" With a sharp intake of breath, he nodded eagerly and began to remove his shirt and pants. I lined up my tools, letting him see me get ready, to heighten his apprehension and anticipation. I walked behind him with my white leather belt. Tracing the buckle down his spine, I gave his ass a quick hit that brought him to kneel straight up. Then I pulled his wrists together in front of him and bound them with rope. Walking back to where he could see me, I let my clothes fall to the floor. I was wearing only a shiny red brocade corset and a satisfied smirk on my face. I could see his cock stirring. An evil grin broke and my eyes lit up. I like it best when I have encouragement.

I blindfolded him, pushed him down onto the bed, whispered into his ear. "This will only hurt a bit." I grabbed his legs and spread them wide. Tying his ankles to the corners of my bed frame, I ran my hands up the insides of his thighs to his cock. I cupped his balls with my hand and teased the length of his cock with my fingernails, alternately scratching and caressing. I then moved his bound wrists above his head and secured them to the head board. Being a Domme doesn't necessarily mean I have to inflict pain... just the opposite with me actually. I enjoy inflicting pleasure only. It just so happens that some people enjoy a certain amount of pain to heighten the sensation of pleasure, as well as making the body ultra-sensitive to any and all touch.

My hands skimmed up his torso to his nipples, to his throat and I pressed gently on his throat while my mouth covered his nipples. Sucking, biting and pulling on each nipple, lapping at his chest with my tongue and teeth – this made his breath ragged and he moaned. I bit down hard on one nipple, while pinching his other one, and he gasped. I left his chest to kiss his neck, lightly nipping up to his earlobe and sucking there, while continuing to skim his skin with my hands and nails. I straightened up.

"Now, I'm going to block out your sense of sound. I want you to concentrate fully on my touch," I said, and with that, placed the earplugs in his ears. He was now blindfolded, deafened and bound. Completely vulnerable to my will... but don't worry, I am a loving, giving Domme. I slicked my hands with lube and took his cock in my hands, sliding both hands swiftly up and up. Then I lowered my lips to his penis, licked his head, and slowly took him into my mouth. Sliding my lips all the way to his base, I rested there for half a second, then tightened my grip and sucked him back to the tip. Taking his head into my mouth again, I locked my lips around the ridge of his penis, letting my tongue play on the underside, making little figure eights and lapping gently. He began to moan and smile. I licked him from base to tip then dragged my teeth lightly up the sides of him. My tongue left his dick to trail to his balls. I took one into my mouth and sucked gently, while my hands gripped his cock to keep it warm and stimulated. I moved further down, pressing my tongue hard under his balls, close to his asshole. Using my shoulders to spread his legs further apart, I let my tongue dance toward his ass. I could feel him stiffen - had he not experienced this before? Oh, the anticipation was mine now... I licked his ass, nipping and biting his cheeks, keeping my hand on his slick cock, stroking him. I thought he was close to coming, and as much as I enjoyed that quick triumph, I wanted this session to last much longer.

I leaned back and reached for my strap-on, and put it on. I took my cock and brought it to his lips. I opened his mouth with my fake cock and put it inside, letting him taste and lick and fill up his mouth with me. He looked absolutely eager to take me in. I slid my cock down his chest toward his and teased his erect penis with mine. He moaned again and began to beg. "Please, please... I want you inside me, Mistress." How I loved the sound of that!

But I needed to drag this out longer. I cannot give him what he wants as soon as he asks for it, you know. So I pulled away from him, and began to suck his cock again, only this time sliding my fingers toward his asshole. I pressed my index finger to his opening and pushed my way in. He bucked slightly and I caressed him to slow down. With even steady movements I massaged his ass with my finger, going progressively deeper. My lips were still on his cock and I timed my sucking with my finger fucking. I was using a small tapered dildo in my strap on, about the width of my baby finger times two. I kissed him gently on the lips, wiping away the sweat on his brow… and placed the head of my cock to his ass. He groaned hard and raised himself to meet me, as much as his restraints would allow. I slid into him slow and steady, my hands on his thighs, urging him wider. Then holding his knees taut against the restraints, I started hitting him harder in the ass, watching his face closely. He was in ecstasy. My hips bumped against his legs, and again I took his cock in my hand. I squeezed him hard and timed my thrusts to my hand stroking him. I slowed and teased him, pulling out, pushing in again, scraping my nails up his dick, sliding my hand down his slickness. After a few minutes of this torture he began to beg again, and this time I obliged. I pushed into him deep and steady, all the way to my base as I stroked him fast and tight. Then I began to pump and he bucked his hips, letting me fuck him like he'd never been fucked before. I was slick with my own wetness. There's nothing I like more than fucking a man.

His mouth opened in an "O" and he gasped, body tensing for that sweet moment before crashing into oblivion, coming hot and hard in my hands. His body rippled and writhed. I pulled out of him and pressed my hand flat against his ass, the heel of my hand pressed under his balls. A comforting feeling. His breathing subsided. He lay limp on my bed, praising me in the incoherent babble of the delirious. I removed my gear, untied his ankles, unbound his wrists, took out his ear plugs… but left the blindfold on. I cuddled up next to him, pulled the blankets up over us. He curled into me like a small child. I took off the blindfold and his eyes were moist.

"Thank you," was all he said as I smiled and kissed his forehead.

"Happy vacation, darling," I replied.

Nature intrinsèque
(ou centre de fille au centre-ville)

Amar

Amar likes to sculpt her stories as she likes to carve wood: with patience and hand-picked tools, and on noble materials. She brings the same care and artistry to her play. When the two meet (unfortunately, not as often as one might like), it produces the kind of story you are about to read.

Speaking of meeting, Amar and I met a long time ago, on the Internet, back before people met on the Internet. I am grateful that she accepted to join me in our leather journey. I am glad that she submitted "Nature intrinsèque (ou centre de fille au centre-ville)". Yes, the whole story is in French. When you read it, you will understand why I thought its poetic qualities were better relayed in the original language. And if your French is rusty, don't worry - the next story is also set on a balcony.

Oh, and Amar does not like to write bios, so now she can see what happens when you leave it to me to summarize your whole life in a few words.

J'ai cherché l'ombre, j'ai cherché le vert en vain dans Toronto la carrée, dans Toronto la peuplée. C'est la canicule, et Queen m'enlise. Le vent m'entraîne, l'idée du vent, plutôt, m'enchaîne, et je la suis. Je tourne à John, puis à Adélaïde, et bientôt j'atteindrai les hauteurs, là où l'air circule, où la ville craque, où la vie des toits sécrète enfin ses jus, parmi les insectes esseulés.

Là, d'au-dessus, je n'aurai qu'à être pour imaginer.

L'ingénieure rentrera de bonne heure, avec un peu du bruit des percussions et des klaxons qui se font souvent contrepoint pour annoncer que la journée officielle tire à sa fin. Elle déposera ses plans, son casque, son téléphone, comme elle le fait toujours et comme le font peut-être ses collègues au même moment.

Je suis à l'attendre dans la jungle des objets rejetés, au 22e étage. Une étagère, des bouteilles vides, des gants de jardin. Une roue de vélo tourne librement par-dessus le garde-corps de ciment, dans un sens, dans l'autre. À travers son mouvement, je survole le lac Ontario. Déjà un building. Je reviens.

Tout près, une empilade de pots à fleurs, où les moustiques viennent pondre et se préparer en petits soldats à sucer le sang des flâneurs, minuscules dans le parc en bas. Puis, une merveille de conception vient faire des manœuvres en vrombissant, les ailes en croix, dans mes pensées. Une libellule métallique. Un hélicoptère moite.

L'ingénieure, comme d'habitude, plie ses vêtements de bureau et les dépose sur la planche à repasser. À peine arrivée, elle se met à nu. Elle enfilera ses grosses bottines de chantier, délacées, pour me rejoindre. Le ciel est clair, le sol est sale, rien n'a encore tout à fait chaviré.

Viens, ingénieuse animale, montre-moi tes chairs tendres. Mon âme voyage et veut trouver un port vivant. Rive-toi à la balustrade tandis que je te desserre. Tu halètes et tu vibres, je te vrille. je fonce fort par derrière toi. Et nous palpons l'horizon.

Toronto la touchante me gagne. Me fait sourire. Comme cette jupe de dame indigne, rouge à pois noirs, qui virevolte entre des antennes sur un balcon là-bas.

Je te reprends. Volte-face, bibitte rondouillette! Tu es si légère qu'une simple évocation te soulève. Et voilà que tu bats des bras. Est-ce pensable que je rie maintenant de si bon cœur en entrant mon poing entre tes cuisses? Tu répands ta réponse en une flaque qui se mêle à la poussière. Ce sera le landau des prochaines générations d'éphémères.

Tu es en général ma pouliche sauvage. Tu es parfois mon zèbre, ma gazelle, mon antilope. Tu es aussi le singe qui grimpe à mon cou, le suricate en alerte, l'araignée qui attrape tout, le ver grouillant, la biche endormie. Nous sommes si peu civilisées, ma petite bête, mon amour.

A Crack of Thunder

Sarah Pie

Sarah Pie is a leatherdyke from Toronto. She says she's more of a do-er (or do-ee) than a writer but in this case "doing good" helped her to rise to the challenge of capturing passion in a net of words.

I met Sarah Pie a.k.a "Maîtresse" to me at various leather events, but we began a journey together a little bit more than two years ago.

I wonder what it says about her that she wrote a balcony scene despite not being a huge fan of heights…

The air was heavy and electric that July evening, so humid that it blanketed both my skin and the raspberries we ate for dessert with fine velvet dew. I could taste the salt as I sucked traces of the overripe berries from her stained fingers; she fed them to me one by one, crushing them over my tongue to release bursts of tart musky juice.

I'm not sure whether it was the dessert or the heat that made me pant. I jumped up from my chair, seeking relief, hoping for a breeze passing by the edge of the balcony, but … nothing. Not a breath. I looked back at the flames of the clutch of candles on the table, stirred by the passing of my half-naked body, and watched them flicker back to stillness.

"Please?" I whispered softly at the dark clouds hanging low over the city in the gathering dusk. Or was it to her? Regardless, it was the sky that answered, with a low rumble barely perceptible over the noise of the traffic. As the last of the sun faded, it stained the underside of the pregnant cumulonimbus the same deep red as her fingers, and occasional lightning echoed the twinkle of the passing headlights.

A rustle and toss of the treetops below announced the arrival of a blessedly cool breath of wind. I smiled my gratitude, and turned to see her eyes gleaming in the dancing candlelight as she leaned back in her chair; she had been watching me intently the whole time. Her gaze reached deep inside me and invoked a wetness that bathed my lips as the rain began to fall at last.

The first drops spattered down and chased scents of hot pavement and of faintly bruised green leaves up to my nose. She stood, and her fingertips fluttered across the skin of my bare back, beating time with the rain, thrumming ever faster as it began to fall in earnest. She thrust my hips against the balcony railing and held them there firmly, as I reached out and let the enormous raindrops splash into my upturned palms.

I crowed with delight as the cold water ran in rivulets down my arms and along the gooseflesh of my flanks. She murmured an approving growl into my ear, pinning me with one hand as she stripped me luxuriantly, inexorably, of my remaining clothing. Two powerful slaps to my ass cheeks wrenched a whimper from my throat until she filled my mouth with her fingers. She continued to spank me, slowly at first, but with a rhythm that matched the urgency of the storm, finally raining blows all over the back and sides of my body.

I suckled diligently, transforming the stinging blows into willing moans and working those precious digits with lips and tongue. From the hardness grinding against my hip, I knew that she was feeling in her cock every attention her fingers were receiving, and I abandoned myself to the task, opening my throat and my heart to her, feeding her arousal.

Once she had taken her fill of my mouth, she slid her hips around to nestle her cock between my burning cheeks, buried a hand in my hair, arched my body back and offered my breasts to the hard rain that lashed at my nipples. She held me tight as I trembled with the effort of the position before lowering me back down and guiding my hands to grasp the railing. "Stay."

Stay I did as she stepped away, though I leaned out sometimes to watch light dance in the sky and raindrops fall past my head. The storm was closer now and the steady rumble of thunder was punctuated by louder noises as lightning split the sky now and then on its way to the tall buildings of downtown.

And then there was a different loudness, this one much, much closer. The perfectly thrown single tail had cracked between my shoulder blades. Although the lash did not touch my skin, the force of the blow knocked droplets of water right off my back. I froze instantly. The small wise instinct in me was already on guard from the storm, so I trembled, but I stood fast.

The first stripe was followed by a shower of others as swiftly as the storm had followed the first drop. I gasped and shuddered and struggled to stay with the sensation. My heart pounded in concert and a low groan built in my throat as she continued. She slowed the pace for more penetrating, deliberate strokes, then accelerated the whip again in a breathtaking flurry that transformed the groaning into a shriek that lay somewhere between delight and agony.

At one point I couldn't help it – my hands flew up in an instinctive gesture of protection, or perhaps I was pleading for mercy? Maybe it was surrender. Didn't matter. She grabbed the nape of my neck and thrust my stinging upper body out into the rain; the falling water was a balm for the rising welts on my back. She pulled me back and, seizing both my wrists, she firmly guided my hands to the balcony railing, holding them in place while she reached behind and gathered a couple of tea lights from the table between her fingers. She placed one on the back of each hand, just out of reach of the raindrops, and repeated her command: "*Stay.*"

She then stepped back and layered burning intensity on my back, my shoulders, my ass, and my

214

thighs in turn. I have always loved being whipped. There is something in the purity of the sensation of the lash that transcends; my whole being becomes elevated, floating. I soaked in the waves of pain, drifted on currents of pleasure, and gave thanks for her and for the animal need that inhabits my body each time I am in her presence.

Having to balance the candles meant I had to broaden my focus from my back, leaving me aware of their warmth on my skin, the darkness of the night, and the fragrance of the pot of basil plants that stood next to me. Had she cut one of the leaves?

She must also have smelled it: after she had finished the tender and deliberate flaying, she looped the whip around my throat, pulled my head back and my body against hers, and crushed one of the leaves under my nose. The spicy aroma filled my senses and left me drooling, indeed, all my mouths were open, dripping.

One of her hands seized each candle in turn, pouring the wax the length of my spine then holding me in place as I bucked against the sudden heat. Her hand swept down my slick flank and cupped my vulva. She laid her fingers along my lips and pressed slowly, squeezing wetness out between them. When they reached my clit the release was immediate, glorious, and somehow ended with all those digits buried deep inside me.

My memory at this point becomes a bit of a blur. I can tell you that the thunder receded, that my thirst was slaked, that her pussy tastes delicious with a hint of fresh basil. Sleeping in the cool air that followed the storm was sweet oblivion.

No Choice

Penny Gyokeres

As a former board member of Mr. Leatherman Toronto and a current founding member of Heart of the Flag Federation, and having had the honour of earning the title of Ms Black Eagle 2001, Penny has enjoyed many inspiring years living within the Toronto leather community. Recently, she was privileged enough to be published in *Best Lesbian Erotica*, 2013 (Cleis Press). She is the owner of Coined Images Photography and hopes to expand into literature and images whenever and wherever they may take her.

Penny is a writer of poetry, music and short erotic adventures, though she would really like to write a full-length novel that sells triumphantly well world-wide so she can retire ridiculously comfortably. Alas, not as of yet. She was born in Toronto, Ontario, and currently resides there and "up north" with her wonderful partner.

I met Penny at various kinky events and fairs, but I had never had a chance to talk to her, except to say, about her pictures, "I love what you do." My first real chance to have a conversation with her was when she was on the Ms. Leather Toronto judging panel and I was there as a contestant. I enjoy her quiet and supportive presence at leather events.

I chose her short story, "No Choice," because it was skillfully written and because I like the kind of kinky story that makes us believe that this is happening for real and show us that it was consensual all the way through.

Y ou have something I want, and I'm going to take it.

You live in the lower East end of Toronto, at Queen and Pape; residential anonymity. The night is crystal clear. The lights are bright on Queen, but as I walk through the smaller streets toward your house, darkness envelops me. Dressed black to blend in head-to-toe gear, I am covert, concealed, as I approach your home. I know you are upstairs, sleeping and silent; you won't be for long. My plan is this: wake you with savagery and take what is mine.

At your back entrance, I slip my knife between the doorframe and lock, slide it in and with a quick snap I am in your world. You cannot deny me; I have been given entrance through the sheer uselessness of your back door lock. That's good for me, we'll see about you. Your home is easy to maneuver; front door, back door and one flight of stairs, not much for the likes of me. Passing through the living room, I smell you. Up the stairs I head: silent stealth.

Your bedroom door opens at my touch and you lie before me. It is a moment of bliss to watch you sleeping, innocent in your slumber, unaware of my threat. Dressed in nothing, your body is everything and I am up for taking all: down to the dredges, you will be mine.

My deft hand pins your mouth shut in a flash because I know you will scream, and you do. Suddenly you are awake, eyes wide and panicked, body tense and defending. A quick gag applied expertly, and you are muffled, like a Doberman with no larynx. My stronger arms flip you onto your stomach and my legs pin yours, offering not an inch of leeway.

Pulling your wrists together, it is such a cinch (excuse the pun), putting your hands in cuffs. Just a quick snap, snap, and you're done: hardly fun. Clawing madly with your hands bound in cold steel, you are making a vain effort to fight me off. Your helplessness is sinking in. I flip you onto your back like you are a hog tied and destined for slaughter. Two more sets of handcuffs, one on each ankle and each to the bedposts, and your legs are spread wide. Your legs are almost as wide as your eyes that were only a moment ago closed in slumber.

"Wanna fuck?" I leer in your ear. Then in the other, "Wanna fuck me?" Snarl is all you can do.

I won't blindfold you; I want you to see me and you and what we are about to do; you with no choice, me with everything. All of a sudden you have nothing.

This makes perfect sense, as I am your robber. Well, actually, not quite. I am your rapist. I just wanted to be clear on that.

I leave you on the bed to consider your position while I take great pleasure in rummaging through your personal items. Flipping the small light on, I ensure that you get to watch as I rifle and meddle and leave you tied and bound, muffled screams coming furiously at me through the gag. Get over it, there is nothing you can do. I smile over at you, proving my point.

What did you think? That all I wanted was your vintage Les Paul, your grandmother's diamonds? Give me some credit you stupid fucking bitch. Not to worry, I'll have plenty of credits when I leave your casino.

You have quieted, succumbing to my rifling, and you are guessing that as long as I am busy with your things, I'll not get busy with you. I think you are getting bored. Time to bring you into the spotlight.

With your body pinned mercilessly, I am directed to my prize.

✝✝✝

Standing over you is a pleasure. The blankets from your bed lie in a discarded pile in the corner. Oh the choices! What to do? My mind is racing with thoughts of you and me and us and coming, well, me coming, and you, honestly I can only hope that you get some pleasure out of this. I think it would make your life a lot easier. I run my black leather-gloved hand over your cunt. You twitch and writhe, rabid at my touch. Oh it is such a pleasure seeing you so mad. Just the pleasure I had hoped for.

You thought I was here to take from you. How wrong you were. In fact, I've got something to give to you. A little, well big, something I have been hiding down my pants for just such an occasion. It's long and hard black rubber, so opposite from the whites of your eyes blazing as I open my fly and you acknowledge my intent. There's no going back now baby, we're in this for the full nine yards. Too bad you seem so unhappy with the whole deal; I was thinking that this would be a lot of fun; you and me and ecstasy, shame you're not having a better time.

Your body is cringing. Your movement is in an as-far-away-from-me-as-possible motion, but there's nowhere for you to go, handcuffed as you are. Right now I love the fact that there is everywhere for me to go, and with my clit racing and my balaclava black as night, I am ready to go.

"Whaddaya say, shall we?" I leer. Your muffled response tells me yes, regardless of your intent, and I am freed into the world of coming and going.

"Where would you like to go?" I ask. "I am coming for you, and you would like to go very far away from me, but this is not an option. We will come and go together, and guess what baby, you do not have a choice."

†††

It's all about me right now, standing, pinching my nipples, leaning over you, rubbing my crotch, stroking my cock, breathing into your ear as I lean and taunt and terrify you. I will rape you. You simply have no choice. I will rape and molest you and leave your bare bones hanging out to dry. By the time I am done, you will have a gaping hole where your heart once was and a record-book orgasm to remember. But only if you are good and listen, and agree with me.

"Do you agree?" Again, your muffled response sounds positive to me.

I lean over your taught, terrified body and run my leather fingers from the tip of your toes to the top of your head. I bring my face in close to your open cunt and smell all the wonders of your deep, dark self. I notice a glisten shining in the light. You are so wet. I remove my right glove and slide my fingers down your lower lips, which are pulsing and straining under my touch.

"Not so bad, eh baby?" I ask innocently. "Sorry, I can't tell if you're moaning or speaking."

I slip a few fingers into you like they were born to be there and I feel your heat closing in. You are the slip-and-slide water ride and I have a ticket. I bring my glistening fingers up for a quick taste: divine. That's my cue as I pull my hand away and kneel between your spread legs. I drive my big black beauty into you. You cry out and move with me. What a pleasure! No, it's not so bad at all, having me rape you. Well, at least now you don't seem to think so. My cunt is pulsing, as I know yours is as it feels and gloriously accommodates the pressure from my eleven inches; rock hard and never wavering from pure dyke-driven power. Your breasts are moving with my rhythm and I grasp your nipples and squeeze with all I've got. I am pushed to the brink. I rock back, pulling my black beauty out, and slam my fist into you. Barreling, pounding, you have no choice, though I don't think you care, I know you are in ecstasy, yeah, you must be because we come together, explode together and are ignited by each other's fuels, dripping and burning through the sheet below.

†††

Dressed in my covert black, I lean back and look into your eyes. Splendid, you are smiling. I remove your gag and say, "I'm free this Saturday, babe, how about a kidnapping?"

With a grin and a yawn you reply, "Brilliant."

Girls Don't Talk about Cars

zibeline

zibeline or z.beline is someone very close to me. I met her ten years ago when I was going through a reflection process about myself and acknowledging my leather identity, and she has been very supportive.

She has been writing lesbian BDSM fiction for about the same amount of time. Under another name, she is a professionally published, award-winning fiction writer, but as zibeline, she usually publishes her short stories on her zbeline.org blog and a few other websites. However, the full-length kinky novel she has had sitting in her computer for ages now might be published soon.

Why did she choose to submit her story "Girls Don't Talk about Cars" to this anthology? "Because, with (female) friends of mine, we always find ourselves talking about our cars. And also because I think of garages as kinky spaces (mmmm, chains!), and because Toronto is where I finally had the chance to fully explore my kinky soul."

The first time she fucked me, it was on the back seat of my own car. I was bending over with one booted foot on the concrete and one knee on the seat, with my bare ass in the air, in the half-lit, half empty garage. After telling me to assume this position, she shoved her rubber-gloved fingers in my pussy and was thrusting into me hard, holding my hair with her free hand. "Come on, back-seat slut, you've wanted this all along, haven't you?" And my answer was lost in moans and lots of fluids on my car seat.

But let's not get ahead of ourselves. You'll first want to know how we met, won't you? When I first moved to Toronto – I moved to Toronto twice, the first time when I didn't know what to expect, and the second time when I was aware of what was awaiting me – when I first moved to Toronto, it was from Montreal. (Yes, that's the hint of an accent you heard and were too well-mannered to comment on.) Most of my friends being Montreal-born, Montreal-raised, they held a sort of funeral wake for me, and offered me farewell gifts and messages that sounded like condolence cards. Those who had never visited

Toronto, or maybe only for a quick visit to the CN Tower, explained to me how depressed I would get in Toronto, and how fast I would want to go back to Montreal. Also they made it feel so far from everything I knew, that for a moment I could have sworn I was moving to Patagonia. Did I ever get bored in Toronto in what I call my first Torontonian age? Of course, I did, just as had in Montreal, but I also enjoyed myself a lot, in ways that I wouldn't have expected, and, also, yes, in the manner you're expecting I'm about to tell you about.

So I moved from downtown Montreal to downtown Toronto, and I must say it wasn't much of a culture shock except that the superintendent would expect me to chat about the slightly milder weather in English (which I discovered I didn't have the vocabulary for), and that I had to walk more than half a block to get wine and beer. Oh, that and the fact that I was paying three times the rent I had been paying in Montreal for an apartment that was half the size of the one I used to live in back there. I arrived with remnants of my past life in tow in a trailer, and managed to start enjoying the new life I would be living for the next twenty-four months, or more if they decided to extend my contract.

The second time she fucked me was with the long chunky wrench with which she had been threatening me (remind me to tell you about this later). She made me lie on my back on the hood of an old car that was awaiting repair in her garage. This time, she had told me to first strip naked in front of her in the middle of the place, so I could now feel the cold metal under my backside. "You're one hot hunting trophy on my car hood, you know," she said, running her hand over my breast, my belly, my bare thighs. And soon, trapping my nipples in booster cable clamps. I moaned heavily under the pain and she laughed a mean laugh: "They're not even my heavy-duty ones." And she twisted them so viciously that I almost cried, then didn't feel like crying at all.

I felt a large object poking at my thighs, and I opened my eyes. She was holding a big stainless steel tool on which she had put a condom – probably an extra-large one, given the size of the tool. She moved it towards my face, and pressed it to my lips. "How would you like to suck this? How would you like to be fucked with this?" I opened big eyes and smiled shyly, but she didn't smile back. She just relocated the object back down and this time pressed it against my bare crotch, first very softly, then, gradually, in a more insistent way. I found myself trying to rub my pussy against it.

"So you do want me to fuck you with this, don't you? You would shove anything in your cunt, would you?" I lowered my gaze and pressed my lips shut. She left the wrench on my crotch, holding it loosely, and bent towards me, playing with the clamps. "Tell me you don't want to be fucked, and I won't insist."

I moaned some nonsense she couldn't hear.

"What? What did you say? I didn't hear you. You want me to quit fucking you? Tell me."

Again, I sighed something unintelligible, even to myself.

"Louder!" she ordered. "Tell me you don't want me to fuck you!"

I finally managed to think and speak. "I can't," I said.

"And why is that?" she asked, moving the wrench in circles on my labia.

"Because it's not true."

But she didn't take that for answer. "What's not true?" she insisted.

"That I don't want you to fuck me. I want you to fuck me. Please fuck me!" I begged, rubbing myself against the tool. And looking at me in the eyes ("Don't you take your eyes off me!"), she inserted the wrench between my labia and pushed slowly but ineluctably. The handle was quite thick and it stretched my pussy cruelly, but I could feel how wet I was, as it slipped quite easily inside of me, then out, then in again. And she kept thrusting, only a bit faster, and harder, until I moaned and screamed and squirted on the car hood.

But she wasn't done with me. She climbed onto me. She took off her coverall from top to waist and sat on my chest. I felt her wetness through the fabric. I tried to move my hands to her crotch, but she pushed them back. With one hand, she held the cables that were still clamped to my nipples and her other hand she put in her coverall, reaching for her pussy. Not paying much more attention to me than if I had been a comfortable piece of furniture for her to jerk off on, she started rubbing herself, still pulling on the cable and my stretched nipples. I moaned, but she kept masturbating. She just smiled at me approvingly when I started moving my body in tune with hers. She remained silent, but I could see she was now breathing more heavily as she kept masturbating. Suddenly, she took her hand out of her pants, just the time to undo the two clamps from my nipples. I screamed and she clenched her thighs around my chest, pressing her crotch on my tortured tits, and I felt a wave spreading from my pussy and I came again, just as she came all over my breasts through the coverall. And then she lay next to me as if the car hood were the coziest bed ever.

But I am anticipating here a bit, aren't I? So, rewind. Back then, I was driving this old fuchsia Buick that I had inherited from my father. Oh, he was perfectly alive, he had just gotten tired of the car. When he gave it to me, it wasn't that colour but a boring beige dotted with rust. This 1992 Buick Le Sabre was quite a good machine, but what can I say, it was an older car. I know, I know, you're not here to listen to me read a used-car column, but actually the car is how this whole story started. Because I had a "mature" car, the first thing I did after finding the closest coffee shop was start looking for a garage. I don't know if you remember, but back then, between the Church Street village and Cabbagetown, on a side street where you could see the occasional rat and racoon, on a corner between a dilapidated Victorian house turned into a pizza joint and a high-rise building, lay a creepy little no-name gas station that was also a garage. If you drove too fast at night, you could miss it, but I certainly didn't miss its name the first time I passed by, the day after my arrival. "Lady Bumper" read the sign, which immediately brought me back to my early disco years (I know, I don't look my age). And, in fact, the place looked like it hadn't changed since the mid-seventies. I mentally took note of the location for future use.

When I stopped for the first time, it was not for mechanical work but for gas on my way to Montreal for a quick visit. Back then, there was still a fair number of full-serve gas stations left, and this one was among them. A few seconds after the bell rang under my tires, someone came out from a door marked "office," an average-sized guy in coveralls and steel-cap boots. When he was closer I realized he was not a guy at all but a wide-shouldered, short-haired woman – although there's a chance she might refer to herself as a butch. She was a hot one. She greeted me and said something that, being a newly transplanted French-speaking girl in an English-speaking environment, I didn't understand, but I pretended I had. I smiled and replied with "Fill it up," which seemed to work.

As she was sticking the nozzle in the pinkness of my car, I watched her strong wide hands in my side mirror. And, also, her round hips and ass that stretched the thick cotton of the coveralls. I couldn't see her face, but from the quick glance I had taken through the car window I knew there was a chance she had been around when "Lady Bump" had first been released (I immediately started calling her Mr. Lady Bump in my head). When she came back to the car window, by the look she gave me, I could have sworn she knew I had been watching her, but she didn't say anything and just walked away, after I paid cash (back then, you didn't expect every place to take debit).

The next time she was about to fuck me, I finally told her my little secret about what I had been calling her in my head from the very first day. "Mr. Lady Bump": she liked it, but decided that I needed to be punished for being so disrespectful to the nice butch who had been taking such good care of my lonely Montrealer pussy. Her wide hand seized the back of my head: "Who gets to name whom here, back-seat girl?" she asked. I gasped, feeling my body melt because I am that easy, and being held that way often has this effect on me.

She pulled harder, and all I could mutter was a feeble "You...?"

She smiled. "That's a good start, but I would like you to show me who you think is the boss here."

I looked at her in the eyes and slowly lowered myself down to my knees, and the lower I got, the hotter it got in my groin lower belly. "You're the boss," I said, wrapping my arms around her hips, my face pressed into her.

She pushed me back. "Not so fast, young lady," she said, and then pointing at her crotch: "You might get some of this later, but only after I'm done with you and I decide so. If I do. Now, I want your face on the floor."

Oh, the sweetness of the order! I lowered myself to the floor, prostrating my body at her feet. She put her boot on my head, pressing my face down on the gas station concrete floor. "Who knew there was such an obedient girl behind the arrogant faces you put on?" She removed her foot from my head and kicked

234

me with the side of her boot. She kicked my arms, my thighs, kicked me some more to open my legs, and hit my crotch with the tip of her boot. I wished she would kick me more down there, but she said: "Now come with me, I have plans for you." I tried to get up, but she stopped me. "Who told you to get on your feet? You're gonna wiggle out of your shirt and skirt, and crawl on the floor like the obedient bitch that you are, and you're gonna wait for me between the blue pillars over there." On my hands and knees I went. The freshly cleaned concrete was cold and hard, but smooth under my flesh – and my knees probably wouldn't get too chafed or stained.

Now, I don't know if you've ever seen the inside of an automobile repair shop, or if you paid any attention. You've probably noticed hydraulic platforms before, that are used so the mechanics can work under the cars. But have you reflected on their full potential? The Lady Bumper garage was equipped with one of these devices, and the blue square pillars were elements of the system. And if the platform could hoist a car, it could surely hold a half-naked girl attached to chains and cuffs and stretch her up until she was on her tiptoes, with a metal bar keeping her legs indecently spread.

Once I was chained up in the middle of the garage, my jailer took a step back and looked at my underwear. "Do you always wear sexy lingerie like that, or am I just lucky?" she asked, staring at me appreciatively. "But unfortunately, not everything can stay." She went to a tool cart and came back with pliers. "Don't move," she ordered. She ran the cold metal cutter all over my body. "I could cut your skin if I wanted," she said, finally cutting my panties on either sides, but leaving me my garter belt and stockings. With the pliers, she also got rid of my bra. "In fact, I could do anything I want with you," she said, running her hands over my naked skin, her face next to my face, her lips almost touching mine. She twisted one of my nipples, watching my reaction. "You are defenceless, and I'm gonna take advantage of it."

She went to a cabinet and came back with an armful of colourful wires of all sizes. When she put them down on the cart, I could see that they were no random wires. They were all neatly attached to a duct-taped handle based on similar size and length. "Floggers," I barely had time to think to myself, before the first one hit my upper back. I screamed, more in surprise than in pain. She laughed. "Ha, you probably should save your screams for when it's worth it. I'm not about to be done any time soon with you." And she proceeded to flog me. She whipped me for a long time, systematically, switching things up often, with all the hand-made floggers she had brought, from the lightest one to the thickest, on my back, on my bottom, on my thighs, on my breasts.

And also, with the tiniest of the floggers, on my open inner thighs. She hit me softly, and she hit me hard. I would try to take it all, then I would attempt to tiptoe away – which, given the way I was hanging from the platform, was rather pointless – then I would just let go and submit to the whipping. She didn't use only her colourful floggers. In addition to her feet and hands and knees and fists, she also beat me with a tiny metal rod that hurt like crazy. She had put the music on, saying that the neighbours were used to her working late on cars and that it would cover my screams. Once in a while, she would put her face next to me, look at me closely, kiss me roughly. "How are you doing, tough girl?" she would ask, probing my pussy as she spoke, finding hot wet flesh.

When she lowered down the platform again, I was a barely conscious piece of flesh in heat. My throat was raw from screaming, and fluids ran down my thighs. I landed on my hands and knees on the concrete floor, my ankles still pushed apart by the spreader bar. Everything around me was blurred, and I had just the vague notion of her positioning herself behind me. And then I felt her cock in my cunt, penetrating me deeply. I heard a moan that I didn't even recognize as my own. She fucked my pussy from behind in long, powerful strokes, holding me by the hair, until I came hard, more than once, and until I had also heard her come.

"I'll be Sir Lady Bump to you," she said when we parted at the end of that night, just before she let me lick her boots.

Back to car matters for a little while — otherwise this story will never end. The story could have ended here, I mean, before all the hot scenes I have already told you about, but obviously it didn't. Cars are thirsty little fuckers and my fuchsia beater was a drunk. I was making regular trips back "home" (which felt less and less like home) to see my family and friends and show them I wasn't dead yet and was not visiting them only to eat their entertaining Montreal brain. Every time I left for a long trip, I would fuel up ("Fill her up" I had learned to say, delighted at the dirty meaning I thought I could see in the phrase) at Lady Bumper because it was the closest place and also because I like to encourage independent merchants, don't I?

Other employees came and went, but the hot butch in coveralls was there most of the time, and I soon learned that she was the owner of the business. By day, the place was a gas station, and at night it became a garage. You could leave your car there and she would repair it overnight, at half of the cost of any other place in town. My fuchsia friend being the old car it was, it also was high-maintenance, so I got into the habit of paying the place regular visits for all the petty repairs that it required, and the major ones too. The word "beater" I learned from Mr. Lady Bump, and she learned the word "bazou" and would use it every time I brought my car to her repair shop. "What can I do for your *bazou* this time, hon?" she would ask and, somehow, the word, when she said it, almost sounded dirty – in a pleasant way. So I would reply in all kinds of funny ways, the double entendres becoming more subtle as my English got better. "I think my radiator is in heat," I would say in a low voice. Or, "I might have an ignition problem." And her response matched my innuendos. "I think you're in serious need of maintenance," or "We need to put the sparks back in those plugs," she would reply in an even lower sexy tone, not missing a beat.

Obviously, we were flirting with each other, but it was as if neither of us knew how to jump to the step beyond the flirt (I had been guilty of this more than once in my life). But I was madly attracted to her and, sometimes, at night, when I couldn't sleep, I would tell myself stories in which she was fucking me behind the counter of the Lady Bumper office.

So one day, I had to bring my car in for something inconsequential, an oil change if I remember right – I think (and can't believe) I said "I need to replace my fluids" as if speaking a second language muffled my whole superego. As usual, I showed up just a bit before gas station closing time, around seven, and left my car with Mr. Lady Bump for the night. Except that when I got back home after the short walk from the garage, I realized I had left my purse in the car, complete with wallet and house keys, and my building's superintendent was nowhere to be found (I suspected he was even more of a drunk than my old car). So I took a deep breath and headed back to the garage in the chilly November evening. (Bear with me, more hot bits are coming up.)

As I was approaching, I could see that the illuminated signs had been turned off. The office, on the right side of the building, was also dark. However, through the high windows of the garage doors, I could see some faint light. Hopefully, Mr. Lady Bump was there, working on a car, maybe mine, I told myself. In spite of the lack of light, I knocked on the office door, in hope that she would hear me. When I didn't get an answer, I went to the garage doors, and knocked a few more times, but the windows were too high and I couldn't get a view of the inside. I went back to the office window. On the side of the office was a glass door through which I could see the garage. I saw my car, with my purse on the passenger's seat, taunting me (although I couldn't actually see it from there). Still nobody was in view. Pausing for a minute, I thought I could hear a faint sound, the sound of water running. I knocked again, harder, but to no avail.

I was left with two choices: either I went back home and waited for the superintendent to sober up, or I found a way to get my purse back. I shivered, feeling the cold fall air through my light coat (all those who say that Toronto is so much warmer than Montreal haven't experienced its harsh downtown winds). To stand and wait for the sexy butch mechanic to come back was not an option. I would freeze to death before she ever found me. I frantically tried the garage doors, but, of course, they were automatically operated from the inside. I hastily went to the office door, but was not surprised to find it locked. I decided the best idea was to walk to the back of the building. Maybe Mr. Lady Bump was there and I could catch her attention, or maybe there was a window of some sort that has been left unlocked, and I could break in and get my purse back. It didn't occur to me that the latter could get me in trouble.

I proceeded to enter the narrow lane between the garage and the chain-link fence that separated the place from the high-rise property next door. A quick dark small creature made its way between my feet and I squeaked. Around the corner I could see light, and it was probably coming from a window, which encouraged me to keep going. When I got to the back of the building, I saw that there was indeed a window with lights inside, but when I pressed my nose to the foggy glass, all I could see was an empty room. An empty bathroom.

A low, menacing voice, and the glare of a flashlight in my eyes: "What are you doing here?"

I shaded my eyes with my hands, but I couldn't see anything. Still, I recognized her voice. "Oh, I'm sorry, this is not what you think. I was looking for you."

The same hard voice: "Yeah, yeah, of course," she said, "And you thought the back of my garage was the place to find me. What were you doing? Playing voyeur while I was taking a shower?" Suddenly, I realized how that must look: me, on my tiptoes, looking through her bathroom windows. But she didn't allow me time to reply. "Come." When she moved aside to let me pass in front of her, I noticed she had a long, shiny garage tool in her other hand. I followed her prudently, confident that we could settle the little misunderstanding. When she took out her keys and opened the Lady Bumper office door, I entered the room as she gestured me, relieved that I was one step closer to my own keys. She shut the door behind me and locked it.

She put the flashlight down and turned on the office lights. Now that I could see her, I noticed that her short hair was still wet and pulled back away from her face. She was not dressed in her mechanic's attire, and wore a black t-shirt, jeans and a leather jacket, but had kept her steel-cap boots. She didn't look angry anymore, had she been before, but... what... slightly amused? However, she still sounded intimidating when she asked: "So, you were spying on me as I was taking my shower?" Before I could say anything, she added: "You're paying me to repair your car, not to give you a free show. Are you the kind of girl who always wants more than what she paid for?" Now we were back on familiar ground. The innuendo.

"No. Maybe I just want the full treatment when I pay for it?" I said with a smile. This time, she didn't let me get away with it.

"You're a wordsmith, aren't you? You like to say it without sounding like you said it, don't you?" She took one step closer to me. "But what is it that you want to say?" She looked at me in the eyes. "What is it that you want to tell me?"

I smiled, trying to think of something humorous to retort. Finally, I said: "I wanted to tell you that I forgot my purse in my car."

She laughed. "Is that all, or is there some cryptic meaning in your words? What does your purse stand for that you forgot to take? What is your car?"

I giggled and pointed to my car through the glass door that separated the office from the garage. "No kidding. My purse is there, look, on the passenger seat."

She didn't look at the car, but looked at me in the eyes. "Oh, really, the passenger seat? I thought you were a back-seat girl." I wasn't sure she meant what I thought she meant. I must have looked puzzled, because she said, in a softer voice: "Okay, okay, let's go and get it," and gestured in the direction of my car with her hand that was still holding the long wrench. She opened the door that led to the repair shop side of the building.

I walked to my car, opened the door and picked up my purse. But when I turned around, I almost bumped into her, and I realized she had been following me, watching me with her almost indigo eyes. I giggled. "Who's the stalker now?" I dared say.

"Oh, it's definitely me," she said shamelessly. "And you're a hot piece of woman." Now, you may call me a sexist, but if a man had said the same thing to me, I probably would have punched him in the face, or the verbal equivalent. Coming from her, it sounded exciting and alluring, especially when she hadn't moved a centimetre, trapping me between her body and the open door of my car. So close, I could smell the scent of her freshly showered body.

I decided not to play the "my pun is bigger than yours" game this time: "You're hot too," I admitted.

She didn't move her feet, but pushed her body forwards, towards me. "You like grease-stained handywomen?" she asked.

"What I like is how sexy you look in your coveralls," I replied.

She put down the long wrench that she had been holding all this time and laid it against my car. She kissed me, and I realized I had been looking for a chance to do this to her for quite a while. But she was kissing me first, and the way she was taking charge of the whole kissing thing, there wasn't much room for me to take the lead anymore. She pressed me against the inside of the car door that was still open, and I felt my body melt a little bit. I melted lots more when she seized my wrists, still kissing me. How did she know? A moan spilled out of my lips. She stopped kissing me and looked at me with a strange look in her eyes. Still staring at me and holding my wrists, she pulled my arm back behind me and pressed her knee between my legs. I gasped and smiled again.

"You may want to take your coat off, my place is heated," she said quietly in my ear. She took a step back. I took off the coat and she tossed it on the front seat, over my purse. I took a step towards her, but she stopped me, putting one finger against my sternum. She looked at my tits and I was suddenly ashamed of my erect nipples, which were pointing through my shirt. "Not so fast, back-seat girl. I've got plans for you. Are you interested?"

I was. "I am," I said. "But you, can you handle me?"

Her only answer was to take back her long instrument, which I learned later was called a torque wrench in English, and, using the tool's end just like the old-fashioned hook they would use on stage during the golden years of burlesque when they wanted to get rid of a bad performer, she pulled me by the back of my neck. With her booted foot, she kicked the front passenger seat shut. Then with her wrench, she made me turn around so I faced the car. She opened the back door and pushed me firmly towards the seat and directed me to bend over. With her tool, she parted my legs then began moving it over my body, like border officers would with their sticks. "Don't you make a move", she said. And off she went to get the thick rubber gloves I would see so many times after that night. You already know the rest of the story now.

Except, maybe, for that special time that I consider the hottest one, when she kept me all weekend long trapped in her garage. I have trouble recollecting all the details, because I was kept in some altered state by the fucking and the beating that occurred, but I know I would do anything to do it again. Would you like to hear bits this last story before we call it a night?

All right, I will tell you what I can remember. So it started on a Friday night. Did I mention that Lady Bumper was closed on weekends? Anyway, it began a couple of hours before closing time. She had asked me to come after work. The minute I set foot in the garage, she ordered me to kneel behind the counter and to strip. I looked at her with big eyes. "Don't give me these eyes, and do as told." Then, in a temporarily softer voice: "Trust me."

I lowered myself behind the counter. It was true that I was really hidden by it, and only someone standing at the cash register could see me. But at the same time, it immediately felt as if the whole street knew I was there. I took off my clothes. She took them away from me and came back with a handful of leather and chains. One leather piece was a collar that she buckled around my neck and fastened to the chain that she then attached to a metal ring that was conveniently screwed to the floor. The other piece of leather was a muzzle that she secured around my head, putting the gag part between my lips.

"Look at the nice garage bitch I've got myself," she said, pulling the chain towards her, forcing me up. Still holding the chain, she kissed me through the muzzle. Then she let the chain go and said "Stay," and off she went to perform her garage duties. For two hours I lay there naked as patrons came and went at the cash register. Sir Lady Bump would chat with them and take their money without paying attention to me or, worse, putting her steel-cap boot between my legs and moving it in circles absently. It took all my will not to moan through the muzzle.

Finally I heard her lock the door behind the last patron. She came behind the counter and looked down at me. "I bet your pussy's wet," she said, forcing her boot between my labia. I was wet, and she smiled. I was already a bit dizzy from the collar, the chain, and the excitement of the whole situation, but I smiled through the haze. She made me stand up. The door was closed and the lights were turned off, but it was still pretty bright outside, and someone passing by could have seen us. They wouldn't have seen my naked body because she made me hold the edge of the counter and bend over a little bit, but they could have seen my head bouncing as she was fucking my ass. Or maybe she fucked my ass the morning after? As I said, I don't remember well, but what I recall is she fucked me and used me in every possible way that weekend, and that she put garage tools where, surely, no mechanic had gone before.

There are two moments I remember rather clearly. One is when she drove me around in the city naked in her pick-up truck's passenger seat. It was late at night and her vehicle was higher than most cars, so people could not really see me, but I could see them and I felt so vulnerable and exposed, sitting naked on a dildo on the vinyl seat, with my wrists handcuffed to the ceiling handle. If someone had noticed what was going on and called the cops we would have been in trouble, but I guess she must have liked to live dangerously, and I consented to it all along. Even when she parked the car in a wasteland in the harbour area and made me give her a blowjob naked in the cold early-June wind. On the way back, she was nice, though; she cuffed my hands together and threw a blanket on me.

The other vivid memory I have involves a power tool. I will never know whether she fucked with my head and I never wanted to ask, but at some point she tied me up in the middle of the garage and blindfolded me, and proceeded to fuck me with a big machine that I couldn't see but could easily hear. Actually, it was so loud that, for all the time it came and went inside of me, its noise was all I could hear.

But it's getting late, and I know you well enough to suspect that you have a fertile imagination. I don't have to tell you all about it, right? You can easily fill in the blanks and picture what she did to me with the funnel, the engine leveler, and all the other tools unknown to me, and how she put the garage creeper to good use, can you? At the end of the weekend, she gave me a long, rough kiss and just said "I like you," before sending me back home all stinky and dirty, dressed only in coveralls.

We had many other good encounters. Thanks to my old car, I had the chance to see her on a regular basis throughout the time I lived in Toronto. Only rarely did we meet outside of the garage, or maybe only for a bite after torrid sex, and I never met any of her friends. She never came to my place although I lived only a few blocks away. But did we ever have hot kinky times when we met!

My contract didn't get renewed. The last time I saw her, she didn't fuck me. I had an empty car tank and a full trailer in tow behind my car. I stopped for gas, and she was there, as usual. She knew I was leaving. She looked disappointed when I had told her, but didn't seem particularly keen to stay in touch. She kissed me goodbye, and that was it. Once I had moved back to Montreal, we exchanged a few emails, but she was not the kind of person to have virtual sex. In the last email I received from her, she told me she had sold the garage and was moving to Northern Ontario. After a couple of years in Montreal, I moved back to Toronto where I still live, but I never saw her again. Sometimes, I picture her with her cock down the throat of a hot country chick in the back room of a small town garage, and I smile.

www.ingramcontent.com/pod-product-compliance
Lightning Source LLC
Chambersburg PA
CBHW052030020726
47501CB00004B/1340